PASSION SPENT

a novel

by

Elizabeth Waterston

CONTENTS

-1-   HURRICANE

A little wind ruffled the lake, too weak to make white-caps but strong enough to break the surface and scatter sunshine sequins over the blue. Dark clouds loomed in the west, though, with a threat of storm coming. Polly slipped out to the lanai and began closing the sliding doors, just in case. Should she go next door and do the same for Elnora Magee? Would her sick, prickly neighbor think she was intruding? Oh, the heck with it, Polly thought, I'm going to look after her a bit, whether she likes it or not.

She reversed the movement of the heavy lanai doors, ready to step out onto the patio strip of cement. Then through the first silver drift of rain, she saw her neighbor Elnora's husband Bill, pounding in from golf, pushing at the patio doors next door, battening down the windows as if he were in charge of a ship at sea. Bill waved to Polly, and each of them turned away, Bill disappearing into his living-room and presumably into a scolding from Elnora, Polly going back to the kitchen and the brownies she had started before that warning little ruffle. Now came the crash of thunder, and the sky was suddenly black, then gray, then invisible as the rain marched across the lake, across the lawn, and flung itself against the little strongholds, the little villas.

Telephone ringing. Carl, of course, alerting Polly, worrying about her: "Is your TV on? There's a hurricane warning." Polly flicked on the television with her left hand; indeed a banner was moving across the top of the screen. *"Hurricane Warnings for south-west Florida."*

"What are you planning to do, Polly? Want to come with us? Fran and I are getting ready to drive inland to the shelter."

Polly had her own hurricane strategy (as Carl well knew). "I'll stay here, thank you, Carl. Under the kitchen table if things really start blowing."

Carl laughed. "Still living in Indiana style, after all these years in Florida, Polly? I figured that would be your answer. But – "

"But you had to ask. I know. And thanks, Carl. Now move! Frances will be getting nervous." They laughed, and Carl hung up with the haste of a man being hustled by a nervous wife.

The banner slipped along the TV screen. "*Hurricane advisory for Manatee County. Residents are advised to follow evacuation routes to the designated shelters. Police are. . .*" And then the screen went blank.

Well, Polly thought, the power went off fairly frequently. No big deal. More serious that the brownies couldn't go in the oven now, with the stove cooling. These breaks were always short ones, and the hurricane warnings familiar enough at this time of the year. Whether the rising wind ratcheted up another notch to hurricane pitch or not, Polly thought, folks would still divide into those who moved inland into the official shelters and those who stayed in the little cement block houses and took refuge in their various and peculiar places – in the bathroom, under a table, tucked up in bed – and no one in either group could convince or convert anyone in the other.

Something was flinging against the lanai door. Yes, trees on the move. Palm trees, the young ones, ripped out of the ground, their close-to-the-surface roots torn unceremoniously from the thin soil. Polly grabbed the morning paper, slid under the sturdy teakwood roofing of the kitchen table, and scrunched there, humping up at intervals to see what if anything could be seen through the blurred windows.

Phone again. (The power lines must be up again, if only briefly). This time her daughter was calling from Buffalo, where the TV was featuring Florida hurricanes (as usual). "Hi, Tansy," Polly said, pulling the phone down under the table, "Nothing really happening here."

"But the TV specifies Manatee County."

"Well yes, but nothing much to show for it right here." (An uprooted bush hurtled past the living-room window. Oh dear, an oleander, flying like a big wet bouquet, out of sight, chased by squalls of rain.) "Really Tansy, don't worry!"

"I bet Carl would have taken you inland —"

"Sure. He called. But it didn't seem worth the effort. This house is cement block. And I've lived through worse in Indiana in the old days."

"Tornadoes. That was different. This is a *hurricane,* mother!"

"Does this conversation seem like a repeat from last September, Tansy?"

"Oh, for Pete's sake!" Tansy had hung up. Just in time too; the phone went dead; power lines down again.

Polly dragged two pillows under the table and settled down, sleepy in spite of the battering wind.

Another fierce crack – maybe the big shallow-rooted palm tree on the other side of the house. Or maybe the even hardier buttonwood between her house and Bill Magee's? The violence seemed to have veered that way, northerly. There was a curious feeling as if the house itself were rocking. Ridiculous! Cement-block house, on a cement pad, with a new hurricane-proof roof – how could it be rocking? She was drifting off to sleep all the same, with a sense of being gently rocked, gently rocked, even in the eye of the storm. Around her the house grew dark.

She woke to rain, driving horizontally past the side window, arrowing less furiously now. Across the grass, next door, a blur of light appeared. A lamp shone out, probably the one Bill had shown her once, saved from long-ago camping trips: a hurricane lamp from northern days when "hurricane" was just a trade name for a kerosene lamp.

The lamp was swinging wildly from side to side. Was Bill signaling her across the rain? He was concerned about her, probably. Then the blur of light moved toward Bill's back door. He seemed to be preparing – good gracious! – to come through the storm to her house.

Neighborly concern shouldn't go that far, surely. He was traversing the grass, hunched right down in a kind of commando crawl, elbowing himself almost flat along the ground.

Up, out from under the friendly table to push the door cautiously outward, Pollly felt it yanked out of her hand. Bill straightened and moved in quickly, tugging the door shut behind him – not concerned after all, or at least not for Polly. "It's Elnora," he said. "I think she's had a stroke. I can't cope!" His usually cheerful face was taut and panicky. "You're a nurse, Polly. Could you come? I'll help you get across."

"Not a nurse, Bill. Not for years now.!"

"She needs help very badly, Polly. I just *can't* cope." He was grabbing her slicker out of the hall cupboard, holding it out for her. She found herself bundled up and out of the door before she could really work up a protest. Crouched down together, they fought their way in that ridiculous crawl through the horizontal push of the rain and the twitching of debris flapping along in the wind, then swayed together at his door as he wrestled it open.

Elnora lay strained on the sofa. It looked as though a terrible hand had swiped down her face, her arm, her side, leaving her in a grotesque arch. She was breathing heavily, but unconscious.

"I can at least make her a little more comfortable," Polly muttered, half to herself, "but she has got to get to a doctor, to a hospital."

"In this storm?" Bill cried. "Even if the weather wasn't so awful, how am I to get a doctor? Our family doctor lives on Cortez, a couple of miles away. There's no one closer. You know there's only the one doctor in the whole development – I can't even remember his name."

"Dr. Switzer; yes," Polly said, "but he's a retired pediatrician, and his house is way at the end of the lake. We'd never get there, and never convince him to come back here, Bill."

"Worth trying, Polly. I'll go, now that you're here. The wind has certainly let up, and the rain – well, it's not that much worse than any storm." He had not taken off his slicker when Polly shucked hers off. His back was turned, and he was out the door, without more argument.

Polly put a strong arm under Elnora and moved a pillow under her head. She reached for an afghan, pulled it up to offset shock; sat by the sofa to wait and see if Bill could rouse Dr. Switzer.

Gerald Switzer (never Gerry) came in with Bill much more quickly than she could have expected. Extra tall, with an extra long bony face, he strode in with a capable take-charge manner, very different from the rather withdrawn appearance of the man who turned up occasionally at social events in the development.

Polly backed away with the deference of her years as a nurse. This was how she had always responded to a doctor's presence. Student nurse, trained to rise in class when a doctor walked in. Probationer, tidying a ward, suddenly silent and motionless when the doctors swept by doing rounds. Registered nurse, in the operating room, efficient and appreciated perhaps but never thanked, never really noticed. Then after marriage, in need of her wages still, night nurse in Emergency, breathless with urgency but halting whenever a resident or intern popped in to check on sudden traumas. So now, twelve years retired from nursing, but still with the old reaction of deferential self-abasement, she stood by Elnora's couch, waiting for instructions. Dr. Switzer turned, automatically addressing her: "Nurse, we must get this patient into hospital. I believe it should be possible now. The storm is subsiding. I'll try – " He pulled a cell phone from his pocket, tried the 911 call. Waited. Then, in surprisingly little time, was giving directions. "Yes: Palm Haven – off Cortez Avenue around 87th street. A stroke victim, urgent. Yes, I am Dr. Switzer." He rang off and turned a tight smile to Polly and Bill. "The ambulance is out this way already. They say most of the streets are being cleared by emergency teams and they hope it won't be too long."

Polly looked out of the window, surprised first at how dark it had become, and secondly at how relatively calm. The storm had indeed spent its fury and was turned now into quite a gentle rain, the wind not much more than the morning's breeze. The little lake was black but peaceful. She could leave now; she did leave, scurrying home to a quiet house, a welcome bed.

The phone was ringing as she shut the door behind her. The lines must be cleared again, just in time for Hal's call. "Mum? I phoned Tansy when I couldn't get through to you. She says you're not ready to evacuate – why not? Everyone says that's the thing to do; there are emergency shelters –"

Polly cut in. " It's really okay here now, Hal. Don't worry. The storm is really over."

"It wasn't a storm, it was a hurricane for goodness sakes! Our TV is still following it and the pictures are horrific."

"Always worse than the reality, Hal, you know that. I really am okay. But would you call Tansy again and tell her the phone lines were down for a while, but are up again now? She may have been trying to call again." She smiled, visualizing his worried look. "Hal, I'm off to bed now. And really, really okay."

So the welcome bed a reality at last.

A day of gentle persistent rain followed. The lake was calm now, silvery gray, curiously empty of birds. The gulls, the pelicans, ahingas, cootes – even the slow-moving mallards – had all fled during the hurricane. The empty lake seemed strange in its motionless suspense.

Polly left the lanai, moved back to the kitchen, and through the window watched Bill coming and going – off to the hospital, home for presumably a bite of lunch; back out the driveway again; home again around four o'clock. Then a procession of people began coming to his door, people bringing salads, pies, casseroles. News of Elnora's stroke had run quickly from villa to villa. The automatic reaction to trouble was help, in the form of food. Polly lost count of the people ringing Bill's doorbell that late afternoon. She watched him pull out again, obviously off to the hospital for the evening; much later, saw his lights swing back into the driveway.

The phone rang. "I need help here," Bill said. "Everyone is bringing me casseroles. The dining-room table is packed already and there are more in the hall. I'm flummoxed by all this stuff. I don't know what to do with them, Polly. Do I freeze everything? Or just put it all in the fridge?"

"What kind of stuff have they brought, Bill?"

"Gosh – pies, casseroles, salads, soup, stew – you name it. Could you come over and have a look?"

Polly answered rather tentatively. "I guess so, Bill. Give me five minutes. I'm not dressed to go out."

Five minutes was more than enough. But the spectacle on the table was also more than enough to stagger anyone. After a moment of gasps, Polly did some sorting – "Freeze this, and this; eat this tonight, it's still hot because it's in that warming ovenette. Eat the salad too. This stew could go in the fridge for tomorrow. And all the rest – have you got room in the freezer?" Yes, she saw when she opened it, there was lots of room. Together they began wrapping the stuff to be frozen in airtight bags.

"Please stay and help me eat it," Bill pleaded. "Stay for supper with me." Polly thought discretion was the better part of valor. She had noticed a flick of light in windows across the street: Millicent Morgan, no doubt watching her coming, and her better-be-soon going.

"No, I'll be on my way home, Bill. Let me know tomorrow what they say about Elnora's progress. You should be hearing something definite by breakfast time."

"Good or bad?"

"I don't know, Bill. Just hold tight and see."

Bill sagged into his chair. "They did suggest that I phone the girls, give them the option of coming to see their mother."

Polly nodded and put on her competent nurse smile. "I'd take that advice, Bill."

"It sounded ominous when they said that."

"No," Polly said. "Just realistic. Either way the girls would feel badly if they didn't come while Elnora is in hospital." He was already moving to the phone by the time she reached the door and went out into the rain.

Her own answering machine was blinking. Two messages, one from each of her kids. She called back, but by now neither one was answering the phone. Saturday night, and they'd be out somewhere, naturally. Polly left soothing updates on their machines. The weather – harmless, unthreatening, nothing to worry about – slid quickly into the story of Elnora's stroke to distract attention from the hurricane. Then she realized ruefully that Elnora's story was likely to stir them up into worrying again about her, on different grounds. She had heard the mantra, "Now, Mother, don't overdo!" so often. It was gratifying, their concern, but a kind of pressure all the same, a reminder of her own age and health problems – all of which she preferred to ignore. She set down the phone, only to start up its ringing again. Bill was calling to tell her that he had called his daughters and that they were both trying to get flights as soon as possible.

"I'll spend the day at the hospital tomorrow," he said. "Maybe you'll come over for supper and help me organize all this food a bit better?"

Polly thought to herself, "I can hear the reaction if this goes on. Every time I cross over to Elnora's house someone will notice." She put the thought into words. "I don't think I'll stay for supper, Bill. Someone would notice."

"What is there to notice?"

"Oh, you know, Bill. You know what they'll begin saying, `His wife's barely at the hospital when Polly – a widow of course – begins visiting him.'"

"That's silly," Bill said. "I don't care about the gossip."

Polly laughed. "Well, I do. Most people in the development don't give a hoot. But those that do can be pretty spiteful. So I'll leave you to your own devices tonight."

Bill laughed too, though not with his old gusto. The long day at the hospital had naturally left him tired out. "I'll call tomorrow afternoon when I get home and face all this food. Maybe you'll change your mind."

"Maybe."

-2-   *TALL BLUE HERON*

Next day the Sunday morning lake lay smooth, a gentle azure piously smiling up at the quiet sky as if neither of them had ever known a storm. On land, the scene was different. The lakeside path had been cleared, but twigs, branches, and bits of mulch littered the grass, waiting for the grounds crew to gather them up when the weekend was over. Polly, pacing along on her morning walk around the lake, saw without surprise a small crowd collecting at the shuffleboard court. The court was too wet to permit play, but people had come together, out of habit and a natural pleasure in foregathering. They greeted Polly with "How's Elnora?" the polite questioning a mask for an uneasy mix of feelings: curiosity, fear, and relief ("Not me, not this time anyway!"). In a retirement community a plight like Elnora's came too close for comfort. Polly gave what news she could and then moved on along the lakeside path.

Two doors before she came back around to her own house, she turned in to visit Carl and Frances. She knocked on the lakeside door, calling, "Safely back, you two?" and was pulled into the lanai for coffee and a pre-church chat. The three friends settled into brightly-covered rattan chairs, put their feet up on the central paper-strewn table, and looked out with a certain irony at the shiny-smooth lake. The sky arched serenely blue, Florida blue, cloudless and innocent. So quick a change from two nights ago! "But you were right to drive inland," Polly laughed. "You can see from the debris how wild it got after you left."

"Well, we each have our own ideas about how to cope with hurricane warnings," Frances answered. "Your way proved okay, Polly, this time, anyway. But next time we'll simply take you by the scruff of the neck and drag you to safety!"

Carl, looking at the quiet lake, spoke the thought they all shared. "Such sudden changes! Peace to storm to peace again."

"Just like Elnora," Frances added. "From –what? – monotonous invalidism to – to sudden total incapacity I guess."

"Except that Elnora's not likely to get back to the peaceful stage, I'm afraid."

So then Fran could ask the crucial questions: What about Elnora? What had really happened on the night of the hurricane? How did they get her to the hospital? What were all these rumors about Dr. Switzer coming out of his antisocial stance and helping Elnora and Bill?

Polly sighed, and told her friends about Elnora's stroke and Dr Switzer's coming through the dreadful weather to help. Then she sat up, struggled out of the comfortable chair and left to get ready for church. "Coming with me, m'dears?" But Carl and Frances preferred to settle in with the Sunday papers and forget the traditional Sunday habit. "No problem," Polly said, and took herself off.

She went to church, came back to a soup-and-sandwich lunch, and then settled in to a good library book. The phone rang, and it was Bill, repeating his plea for help at supper time. "I just can't cope with all this food. And there's more today, Polly. Please. Please come over and organize it all again."

She hedged. "Aren't your daughters coming today? They should be able to sort things out for you."

But the answer was no; his daughters had not been able to get flights this morning; they wouldn't be in until almost midnight.

Polly thought a minute and then said, "Okay. I'll come over. I'll find a casserole dish and put a lid on it and carry it in a tea-towel as though it was hot."

"Why on earth?"

"Just a notion. When I come over to your house again, people will notice. There are plenty of eyes behind the Venetian blinds. If I come over empty-handed, they'll think you've invited me to have supper with you. Tomorrow the whole development will be buzzing."

"That's crazy! What's the matter with everybody, all this tendency to gossip?"

"People haven't got a heck of a lot to think about," she answered. "We'll do it my way. Anyone keeping an eye on us will just think I am adding to the supplies that will keep you going while Elnora's in the hospital. Okay? Give me five or ten minutes and I'll be there."

Bill's kitchen was by now almost as chaotic as the rest of his house. From the front door Polly glimpsed the mess in the living room – the sofa where Elnora had been lying still heaped with afghan, pillows and blankets, and the rest of the room strewn with newspapers, shoes, a jacket, a chair pulled into the middle of the room – a general look of having been stirred and tumbled. But the kitchen table was clean, and Bill had begun to organize supper. It was the best meal Polly had had for ages: delicious clam chowder, just needing heating; a veal stew complete with tiny new potatoes; a broccoli casserole; and such a choice of pies that she and Bill each sampled three. She could barely move when it was over, but she firmly declined the invitation to stay and watch the Sunday night television comedies. "Off I go!" she laughed, and off she went.

At six next morning, Polly, watering her garden, looked with joy at the storm-free world. Mist rose gently from the lake. Two quiet ducks, safely returned, glided out from the shore. The flowers, pulling themselves upright, stood in barbaric autumn color: marigolds, purple salvia, scarlet geraniums, all as if there had never been a hurricane.

Bill's screen door clicked. One of the daughters – Loretta? Lorraine? – they looked alike, and they rarely visited; hard to know which one it was. "Hi," the young woman said. "Polly – isn't it?" She stuck out a hand, smiling vaguely. "You've been so kind to

Daddy, so he says." She stepped gingerly through the wet grass to join Polly. "Lorraine is coming this morning, at – let me see – at ten-forty-five," Loretta (yes, Loretta) said. Water rose from Polly's hose in a rainbow; but Loretta of course was in no leaping mood. She said in a small voice, "They sent for Daddy and me last night from the hospital just after I arrived. They say this is a critical point. What does that mean, um – Polly?"

"Not sure." And Polly wasn't sure how much this fuzzy-headed young woman understood about her mother's case. Tentatively she said, " Maybe they fear another incident."

"Another stroke?" Perhaps she wasn't as vague as she appeared.

"Just maybe, Loretta. But you need a cup of coffee. Come on in."

Sitting at the kitchen table, circling the mug with shaky hands, the young woman proffered a tentative question. "Could one of us possibly stay in your spare room, Polly? Either Lorraine or I? Mother's spare room is impossible. Chuck full of everything under the sun – "

Polly said, "Of course. The beds are made up, and there's a bathroom next to the bedroom. It's the same setup as your dad's place."

"Same but not the same," Loretta's drawn face pulled into a half smile. "Daddy's house is a mess, poor dear." Her glance swept around Polly's not-so-tidy kitchen. Not a mess, but not spick-and-span either. Polly's whole house was cluttered – there was no other word for it. She had bought this place "fully furnished", and then had brought her own dearest things: the Danish recliner, grandmother's Victorian love seat, a couple of little tables. Loretta eyed the scene and said tactfully, "Such a homey house, Polly!" Then she tried another smile. "We'd really be glad of your hospitality. We could let you know whether it would be me or Lorraine."

"Room for both, if you like."

"No. One of us should stay with Daddy. And I'd better go back now and get his breakfast." She paused at the door. "Aren't you going to have any coffee yourself?"

But this was Monday, and Monday morning was the weekly coffee get-together at the community clubhouse. "I can only take one cup per day, Loretta," Polly admitted.

Time to go along to the clubhouse. Loretta took the hint and trailed back toward her father's villa. For Polly, there was just time to join her own little circle at their special table: Carl and Frances, Irma Beaton and the Elricks, a younger couple (that is, people in their early sixties) who had become part of the regular circle this year. They all collected their coffee and doughnuts and settled in at the table. But where was Irma? "She said she was coming when I spoke to her last night," said Frances; but the others sighed and remembered that Irma was becoming rather forgetful, so Polly slipped out to the office and phoned her. Fluster, fuss of explanations – but basically "I forgot. You know my short-term memory, Polly! Save a seat for me and I'll come right away."

Meanwhile various neighbors drifted by, officially to ask about Elnora, but the Monday morning questions were in fact mostly about Bill, about his daughters' arrival – very little about Elnora herself. Everyone would have had a lot to say about an ordinary sickness, even about a heart attack or cancer, detailing probable length of treatment, and what could be done to help. With a stroke, everyone shied away from the thought. Such a severe stroke too; most of these people thought with dread about the possibility of long-time dependence, irreversible debility.

The talk shifted to condominium affairs. There was a call for people to volunteer to act on the steering committee, organizing social events. This year it was time to redecorate the club house, so a good committee was specially important. "How about you, Carl? Could I nominate you?" Irma asked as she slipped into her place at the table.

Carl laughed. "Too busy." He turned to Ginger Elrick, one of the newcomers, but she raised her hands in protest. Maybe next year, she promised, but this year she and Jackson were still too busy settling in, getting to know life in the community. "Just surviving the hurricane has been quite an initiation for us."

Carl smiled at her. "I'll ask again next week – you won't be such a newcomer by then. Time condenses here." Then he gasped, "Holy mackerel! Look who's coming across to us!"

It was Dr. Switzer, following an unaccustomed path across the room, stiff as usual, but offering a thank you to Polly for her quick actions on Friday night, hoping she wasn't too tired, saying, "That's all right then," and striding back to his own favorite table in the back corner. Frances exclaimed, "Well! That's the first time he's been known to speak to anyone except the Malones. Everyone else has given up trying to be friendly to him, or so I've heard."

"He wasn't friendly when Bill dragged him out to see Elnora, but he was certainly efficient," Polly replied.

The conversation swung back to the question of redecorating the club house, and finding a good committee to look after the job.

On the way home, Polly strolled with Carl and Frances along the lake path. "Come in for a minute," Frances said, as Carl left them to go to the corner store for the newspaper. "Come and tell me what's really going on with Bill and his daughters."

Polly obliged with a quick sketch of Bill's dilemma over the food, and Loretta's manner of inviting herself to stay in Polly's house, leaving Lorraine to cope with Bill's messy housekeeping. She laughed at herself. "And I make fun of my neighbors for their gossiping! What a bunch I'm unloading on you, Fran!"

"No, no," Frances said. "This is not gossip. It's information."

"Sometimes it's hard to distinguish one from the other!"

The difficulty of distinguishing seemed clear again when Carl came in with the local paper, full of fragments of reporting about how people experienced the hurricane. "Not much hard news there," he said. "Our kids up north, watching the weather channel probably got a better idea about what actually did and did not happen."

Polly stood up. "That reminds me. You know Tansy always phones on Monday morning, after the Coffee-Cupper, to hear the latest Palm Haven gossip, and generally catch up. I'd better get back home to be there for her call."

"Tansy is a marvel," Frances said. "I'm so jealous! If we didn't phone our boys we would never know whether they are alive. More to the point, they'd never know if we were still around!"

Carl pretended to scowl. "Come on, Frances, it's not that bad! You know we came to Florida to get away from too much detail about the boys and their wives and their children and their jobs and their friends –"

"And their wrong-headed opinions, in your view, Carl!"

Polly smiled at her friends, ready to be amused by their mocking version of their family feelings. Young Lars and Norman Andersen might not phone regularly, but they made unexpected flying visits to Carl and Frances – more than could be said of Tansy and Hal. Ah, well, to each his own. The younger generation were various in their ways, and one had to accept what one got in this world. Polly pushed herself out of the deep chair, picked up her coffee cup and got ready to move on home.

On the cement slab outside the lanai door, a great blue heron stood like a statue. Almost four feet tall, it stood with its beautifully colored body poised on wrinkled, elongated legs seemingly too thin for such a burden. It turned its head right and left to watch Polly emerging from Fran's house. Four years ago, when Polly had first come to Florida to buy into a retirement community, a dignified heron just like this one had walked toward her, around the corner of a house for sale, just as if it had been a welcoming committee. She admitted now, with rueful self-mockery, that the heron had played a big part in her decision to buy that particular villa, from among all those on offer. The heron on Fran's patio was no doubt not so much making a friendly call as hoping to be fed (though everyone was warned not to feed them, for fear of making them dependent on the humans who shared their environment). Polly told this one, "Sorry – nothing for you!" and moved quietly toward the lakeside path. The heron stalked away with stately dignity. Its gait struck her as comically like Dr. Switzer's, when he walked across the clubhouse this morning.

Fran called after her, "I have something serious to talk to you about, Polly. But I'll wait until this Elnora business settles down. You're probably still on call to help Bill if things get worse."

Things got worse. Things got as bad as they could be. Bill and Loretta and Lorraine virtually moved into the hospital for the next two days. Then the expected end came: a second stroke, fatal this time. Polly could guess what had happened, from the sight of the three of them, disconsolate, slowly getting out of the car and going into the empty house. Should she go over? "They know I'm here. They'll ask, if there's anything I can do for them."

Two hours later, Loretta trailed across the grass, wanting to change her clothes, to get into the dark dress she had brought "just in case." "May I stay with you still for the next few days, Polly?" she asked. "Lorraine and I don't get along at the best of times, you know. It's bad enough arranging everything for the funeral without arguing about every little thing: what hymns, who's to speak – everything! It's better if we stay away from each other as much as we can."

It seemed to Polly not a good sign for the future if the girls couldn't even agree to adjust to each other for the next few days, but there was no point in saying so. Loretta was a harmless guest, not very interesting and not very helpful, but you could forgive a lot right now. "I won't see too much of either of the girls in the future anyway," Polly told herself hopefully.

Regardless of their differences, the two young women took off for the beach together the next day. Lorraine had rented a car at the airport when she arrived, and the girls decided to get their money's worth out of it. "Poor dears, they need a little pleasure," Bill said. "They have to get back to their own lives right away, so this is their only chance for the beach. I guess I can do all the arranging for the funeral anyway, Polly. They are both too nervous to be much use in making decisions anyway."

Bill set off to the church, where he and his priest settled all the questions about the funeral service, to be held at eleven o'clock on Saturday morning. An hour later he came back to his house, slow and dejected.

Late in the afternoon the girls returned from the Gulf shore in time to enjoy some of the wonderful food still flowing in from the neighbors. When Loretta came over to Polly's house for a clean shirt, she insisted that Polly come and "help eat up some of the stuff." No harm in that, Polly thought; could anyone object if she enjoyed the food the neighbors had provided for Bill and his daughters, since she in turn was putting up, and putting up with, said daughters? Neither of the young women had made any perceptible effort to straighten up their mother's belongings. No harm in that, either; that job could wait for a while.

Later still, it was Lorraine that came over to Polly's house to spend the night. "My turn, I told Loretta," she said. "Time for her to talk to Daddy for a while. Is that okay with you, Polly?" And then, before Polly could do more than make a polite agreement, "We'll both be at the funeral parlor tomorrow in case anyone comes for a visitation. We'll leave most of mother's things just as they are until we come back at Thanksgiving. And about Saturday – Loretta and I decided to ask if you would sort of run things after the funeral service. The ladies' auxiliary of the church are organizing the food for a little reception. But Loretta and I figure you will know all the people there, and we won't. So would you sort of take charge?"

"No, thank you," Polly said. She had a reputation to maintain, a reputation for not being maneuvered into accepting jobs she didn't want to do. She certainly had no intention of acting as hostess at Elnora's funeral. Lorraine looked taken aback, started to argue, and then thought better of it. "Okay," she said. "No problem. We'll manage. I'm sure that once things get started you'll want to pitch in and sort of circulate, even if you're not really in charge. Okay?"

"No," Polly said. "This has got to be your show, Lorraine. Yours and Loretta's. You'll see. You'll find you're managing fine on your own."

Lorraine just smiled, and as if by mutual agreement she and Polly both started down the hall to the bedrooms. "Good night, my dear," said Polly, thinking, "Poor dears, of course they're upset; but they'll see that they have to take charge when the time comes."

Next morning Polly phoned Carl and Frances to ask if they could go to the funeral together, although she suspected that they would not be going at all. Suspicions confirmed: "We don't go to funerals," Carl said firmly, and Fran could be heard in the background saying, "That's right."

"I'll ask Irma to give me a lift then," Polly said. "No sense filling up the parking lot with extra cars."

-3-   *EIGHT GULLS WHEELING*

Just after eleven o'clock on Saturday, Polly walked up the central aisle of Sts. Peter and Paul with Irma Beaton. They slipped into a seat, noting with some surprise that Dr. Switzer and his friend, another doctor named John Malone, were sitting in the pew ahead of them. "I've never been in Catholic church before," Irma whispered and she reached for Polly's hand. Tension tightened her grip, and Polly quietly covered the little hand with her own. "I have – often. My son Hal married a Catholic, you know."

There was a slight horror in the answer, "No, I didn't know."

"Sure," said Polly, shifting from holding into patting the hand. "Three of my grandchildren are being brought up as Catholics."

"Your son *turned?*" There was a Baptist dismay in the question. Polly said, "At least they all go to church. More than my Protestant grandchildren do."

There was a little pause, while Irma perhaps reviewed the lessened church-going of her own non-Catholic offspring. "Well – " (the hand relaxed a little under Polly's) "we shouldn't be thinking of such things right now, I suppose. Poor Elnora. It's all the same to her now."

At which uncheerful thought Polly sighed and let go of Irma's hand. Up in the gallery a little boy chorister began to sing "Panis Angelicus" and the procession of clergy and mourners moved quietly up the aisle. Bill's two daughters were with him and an older man, presumably his brother. Indeed there was so strong a resemblance that they might have been twins. Bill and Elnora had never talked much about their families. With the focus on Elnora's health all through the five years that they had lived next door, they had never exchanged much information of any kind with Polly and the other neighbors. Bill had always smiled in a friendly way; it seemed as if Elnora had never smiled at all.

"Requiem," the choir sang, and "Light perpetual," the priest intoned. Then, more cheerfully, "The Magee family hope you will all come across to the Parish Hall for a little reception. Bill and his daughters asked me to emphasize how much they hope to see you all there."

Irma said, "I can't take any more of this, Polly; I'd like to go home. Can you get a lift with someone else?"

"No problem," Polly answered. "There are lots of people from the Haven here. I'll be okay."

"Then I'll see you Monday, if not before," Irma said and left Polly to cross over to the Hall by herself. As she went through the big doors, and before she could protest, she found herself seized by Loretta and Lorraine and pulled out of the group entering the hall, up to the little dais at the front where Bill was standing. "We know you won't really mind helping us," Loretta said. "Just tell us the names of people when they come up – just so we know who's who." It would be rude to argue. Polly stood straight and did her job, maneuvered into position between the two young women. She hated this kind of ceremonial occasion. Even when first Tansy and then Hal had married she had thoroughly disliked the receiving-line ritual. She knew her cheeks must be flushed as she fought down irritation. She thrushed her fingers through her short gray curls, smoothing them as well as she could. Standing in her straight-cut cotton suit beside Loretta and Lorraine in their long floating dresses and their long floating hair, she felt herself to be miles out of style, besides bring miles out of place. The people she knew smiled at her amiably as they came through the receiving line; nevertheless she felt she had been put in a false position, as if she were a special friend or a member of the family. The line moved on, and Polly settled with resignation into the work of announcing names when she remembered them, and devising ways of disguising her lapses when the memory failed.

The reception seemed to last forever, and yet it was barely one-thirty when the last visitors left. The women of the church auxiliary insisted on boxing up leftovers for Bill to take home, so once again there would be a sorting job to do back at the house. While Bill and his daughters gathered the boxes, Polly slipped out the door, tired and more than a little cross at the end of the performance. To her surprise, Dr. Switzer was waiting for her. "John and I will give you a lift," he announced. "I heard Mrs. Beaton say she was leaving you to your own devices."

Without thinking, she found herself saying, "I didn't expect to see you here, Dr. Switzer!" He nodded formally. "I don't go to funerals as a usual thing, but I did think the Magees needed all the support they can get. Bill especially. He's had a very long siege with his sick wife. We play golf together sometimes, you know." Polly had not known, but of course she hardly kept tab on the golfing groups. He had changed the subject. "I was telling John here that I'd be glad to have a chance to speak to you. I feel I owe you an apology for treating you so brusquely on the night of Elnora's stroke."

"All forgotten!" she smiled as she climbed into the car. "It seems ages ago, anyway. So much has happened since that night. And look how the weather has changed."

"That's Florida weather," he agreed. "Sudden trauma, quick recovery!"

John Malone laughed at his friend. "You see we can't get away from medical language, even about the weather."

The car pulled into the driveway between Polly's house and Bill's, just in time to see Loretta and Lorraine carry their beach equipment out to the rented car: umbrellas, beach chairs, towels, a picnic hamper. The young women ran back into the house with the obvious intention of changing into beach clothes and taking off for a picnic supper. "Is Bill going with you?" Polly called to them. The answer was no – too depressed to feel like an outing. "But for us, it's our last chance for sunshine before we go north again. We're both leaving tomorrow."

Polly turned back to say goodbye and thank you to Doctor Switzer for the ride home. She found him grim-faced. "Not very concerned, are they?"

Polly answered slowly, "No." Then she added, "Maybe it's just as well. My own son and daughter sometimes seem to me to be too serious, over-concerned about everything." Into an awkward silence she inserted an awkward question, "How about you? Would your kids take off to the beach in a case like this?" Then she realized she didn't know whether the doctor had any offspring. His answer was noncommittal. "I have no idea how they would react to my death. Or to any of my doings."

His friend remonstrated, "Come on, Rusty, they're not that unconcerned!" but Dr. Switzer remained chilly.

. Feeling she had been graceless, Polly said, "Well, all any of us can do is live our own lives, right?" At this both men smiled, then said good afternoon and waited till she had opened her own door before driving away.

Polly went through to the lanai, pulled back the vertical blinds that she had drawn against the sun when she left for the funeral. She stood for a while watching eight gulls wheeling over the lake. They swooped and flew, dived and settled, then, restless, swooped up again. Restless, restless. Beautiful in their own way, but unsettling as they winged through the restored peace after the hurricane.

A strong warm wind pushed against Polly as she walked around the lake to the club house on Monday morning. Coffee-Cuppers was being held again, already. The week had gone unusually quickly. As she mounted the stairs people were asking, "Have Bill's daughters left for home?" "Aren't they a pretty pair of young women?" "Wasn't it fortunate that they could come down to help him?"

Polly, who early this morning had changed the tumbled sheets in her spare room, brought Fantastik to work on the sticky dresser, cleaned the tub and wiped up the general mess in the bathroom, answered a stony "Yes" to all questions. She lined up for her coffee and doughnut and fended off more questions and comments about Bill and his family with noncommittal answers, until she could slip away to her own customary table. Unexpectedly, Dr. Switzer came over to stand beside her in the lineup. He announced that he would be phoning her at lunch time, "if convenient," and then dropped out of line and out of sight. His gait was indeed rather like that of the tall gray heron.

Irma, Fran and the others had obviously not noticed, or else they were being uncharacteristically tactful.

"You got home all right yesterday?" Irma asked when Polly reached the table, cup in hand. "Sorry I left you in the lurch, but I had really had it, with all that chanting and incense and everything." Then she added, "I think I'll ask Bill for dinner later this week. I just hope he wasn't offended by my not going to the reception."

"Of course he wouldn't be," Carl scoffed.

Irma's comment had opened a gate, and another woman at the next table, overhearing her, cut in, "I had the same idea. I plan to ask Bill to dinner in a few days too." Polly foresaw a new era, with Bill the object of dinner invitations rather than gifts of food. Neighborliness again, though it was interesting that this special brand of neighborliness seemed to affect the single women most strongly. As if to throw shame at her thoughts, Carl turned to Frances and said, "We'd better ask him over too, don't you think, Fran?"

Everyone liked Bill, though no one knew him particularly well. He was good-looking, and he had maintained a pleasant manner all through the last three years of his wife's increasingly bad health. He was attractively slim: probably having to cook for himself had protected him from the "down-slipped chest" of most men his age. Golf had been his only recreation and escape. Now there was a tacit agreement that Bill should be shown every possible friendliness, enough to make him want to stay on at Palm Haven and be welcomed into warmer membership in group activities than had been possible before. The table talk returned to questions and comments about the funeral details. Everyone seemed in good spirits, the usual aftermath of sadness.

With a sharp change of tone, Ginger Elrick announced, "I've thought over the business of the steering committee. I've decided I might indeed run."

"Good girl!" Carl cried, obviously pleased that no one had put any more pressure on himself to take on the job.

Ginger continued, "I've always played a very active part in neighborhood affairs, wherever I was living. I'm certainly interested in the question of redecorating the clubhouse, and glad to throw in my two cents' worth."

So the little group put their heads together and drew up a mini campaign to get her elected, an easy enough business, since no one particularly coveted the steering committee job.

Drifting homeward after Coffee-Cuppers, Frances sounded equally vigorous. "I'm restless," she said. "I feel as if we should be doing something other than sitting around, enjoying life, going to the occasional movie, going out for the occasional meal, watching the lake."

"Watching the gulls and the pelicans. I know," Polly agreed. "Not a very pointed life, is it?"

"That's right. Life's so short, and we're vegetating, Polly. We've got to get into some activity, preferably outside the complex. I'm getting condo-bound. I can't get Carl to do anything with me. It'll have to be you!"

"Well, you know me, Fran. I'm still enjoying retirement. The joy of laziness."

"I have one idea I'd like to float by you, though," Fran persisted. "How about getting into Meals-on-Wheels? I could drive, and you could run the food in to the patients. We'd be doing something useful, delivering food to shut-ins."

Polly tried to laugh off the suggestion. "Gosh, I think we're about ready to be on the receiving end, Fran!"

But Frances was serious, and she pushed for a serious answer. Polly said slowly, "I mean it about not being ready. I've been here almost five years, I know, but I still feel I'm just settling into the warm Florida life. I'm still relishing the idea of not having any duties I have to perform. Not being responsible for anyone but myself. Not sticking to any schedule except ones I set for myself."

Frances shook away her answer. "No kidding, Polly, I think Meals-on-Wheels would be a good idea and we could work together well. We ought to be doing something useful."

Polly looked out at the shining lake, where six mallard ducks were placidly floating. "You sound like my mother," she said. "She used to quote a poem to my sister and me:

`So here has been dawning another blue day.

Think! Wilt thou let it slip useless away?"

"I know," Fran laughed. "My mother too. Her favorite was something about leaving footprints in the sands of time." More seriously, "Our mothers were right, though. Admit it!"

"I gave up worrying about mother's ideas twelve years ago," Polly replied, "when I quit nursing. You remember I spent the last eight years before my pension came due doing utterly useless work as a file clerk."

"But keeping files is useful, surely!"

"Not those files. In fact they were all scrapped the year I retired. When the hospital went onto an automated record-keeping system they realized the old stuff simply wasn't worth converting."

"You're trying to get me off the track," Fran protested. "But I won't give up!"

Carl laughed. "She won't let you off the hook, you know. When Frances gets an idea she gets it hard. Watch out, Polly! "

Polly retorted, "Why doesn't she talk you into going on the Meals-on-Wheels trips with her, Carl?" but Carl just laughed again and said, "Don't think she hasn't tried to co-opt me. But I'm safely committed to tennis and golf, and serving on the architectural committee and singing in the chorale; much too busy to have time for community service."

Fran shook her fist at him and threatened, "I'll get you some of these days! You too, Polly. Just wait and see. You'll get over this yen for irresponsibility before too long."

But Polly reiterated, "Not just yet!" and started back toward her own undemanding house.

She was on edge, and no puzzle why. She was waiting for Dr. Switzer to call. What for? What about?

His call came on the dot of twelve noon. ("Lunch time," obviously, was not a vague term.) He had a proposition to make, he said, but first an explanation. He and Dr. Malone had been asked many times to fill in with local medical people, doing some of the jobs that were getting harder and harder to fill. "Cut-backs, you know." They had finally agreed that they could each give two days a week to the "well-baby" clinic in east Bradenton. They had been asked if they could each bring a nurse to fill a further gap: "Cut-backs, again, affecting all the medical fields."

The explanation had taken so long that Polly was ready with her defense when the proposition eventually came. Could she assist him at the clinic on Tuesdays and Thursdays? Just in the afternoons?

The answer was swift, "Sorry, I couldn't. Not possibly."

A moment's silence. "But you're a nurse," he said.

"Not any more. I'm simply not interested."

"Not interested in public health? Impossible!" The voice was icy.

"Completely possible," she countered, "You will have to find someone else."

"Thank you, I will." The phone clicked sharply into silence.

Polly thought, "Maybe I should have explained to him, as I did to Fran, that I'm just not ready yet to be anything but a retiree." Then a second thought: "If I explained, he'd probably just wait a week and then ask me if I were ready yet. Better this way, even if he thinks me heartless."

Life resumed its routine: just time for a few minutes in the garden before Tansy's call was due. The tall heron was standing in her way, immobile. It turned its shiny eye to watch her but otherwise made no sign it acknowledged her existence. She moved steadily up the path, and the heron finally stalked away with a queer military stride, the dark epaulette at the top of its wing adding to the effect of a military presence. "Bye, bye, Charlie!" Polly said, watching the bird's dignified retreat.

She heard a quiet laugh. Bill was standing in his driveway, about to get into his car, but waiting for a word with her. "Had a call from the girls to say they both got back safely. They asked me to thank you for taking them in and being so kind to them."

"That's okay, Bill; I was glad to help." Polly pulled the house key out of her pocket and turned to go in.

Bill had more to say. "The girls are coming back at Thanksgiving, not so very long away now. They say I should just leave their mother's things until then, and they'll do the sorting out. They also said to ask you to plan on spending Thanksgiving with us. They want to take you and me out somewhere nice for dinner."

Polly had to hustle for an answer. "I think Tansy is coming, Bill, and that will mean we go to her mother-in-law at Clearwater."

Bill just said, "Well, we'll see. I don't want to disappoint the girls, and they were both insistent on my lining you up to do something nice together." He opened his car door. Feeling a bit guilty, Polly asked if there was anything she could do for him in the meantime. He shut the door again, smiled sheepishly, and answered yes, there was something that he had meant to ask her, but had felt perhaps he shouldn't. It was a question of garbage, he said. The garbage men would only take two big bags at a time, and he had much more than that. Bill pointed back into his carport, at a row of green garbage bags. "Could I put two of them into your garbage can tomorrow morning?" Of course Polly agreed; he smiled, shut the car door and was off to his golf game.

Hurrying in to pick up the summoning phone, Polly found herself telling Tansy, not about the garbage proposal but about the invitation to spend Thanksgiving with Bill and his girls. "Now don't you get involved, Mother," said Tansy. "You'll find those so-called girls unloading all their responsibilities on you."

"No way, Tansy. You know my new creed: 'No duties. No responsibilities.' I was just telling Fran and Carl —"

But Tansy was not to be side-tracked. "Yes, I know what you say. But just promise me about what you *do*. Fend off those Magee girls or you'll be sorry!"

Polly laughed and turned the talk to other things. Tansy's job, the new tiles she had ordered for her kitchen.

Talk about the weather. "Perfect here in Florida."

"Lucky you! There were a few snowflakes in the air here last evening."

"Well, that's Buffalo! After all it's nearly November. I remember when you and Hal were little I often had to put snowsuits on you, underneath the Hallowe'en costumes."

"How well I remember!"

Then Polly slipped in a question about the possibility of a visit at Thanksgiving. ("Because I did lie to Bill, Tansy; I told him you were coming here.") Tansy temporized. She couldn't say for sure; she and James had half-promised a friend in Rochester to go for a visit there. "Better see if Hal is available, Mother. He'd protect you from those Magees as well as I could."

They both knew the reality under all this: Tansy would not be coming for Thanksgiving, and the odds of Hal's coming were small too.

-4-   *BEGONIAS*

Millicent Morgan, the lady across the road, phoned on Wednesday to invite Polly to dinner. She intended to invite Bill Magee too. "He shouldn't be alone too much, you know. Such a difficult time." Polly did not propose to become a major helper for Bill, however. They had never been more than good neighbors, never talking seriously, only exchanging a few words over the years, about Elnora's health, about the mailman, the paper delivery, or the weather. Polly had no intention of becoming seen as an appropriate dinner companion, someone to be invited along with Bill during this "difficult time." Since Mrs. Morgan had never made any gestures of friendship to her before this, she said, without much compunction, "Sorry, I promised Carl and Frances Andersen to go out with them to the Sea Food Shack for dinner tonight."

"But I didn't mean tonight, particularly. Would tomorrow be better?"

Polly, foreseeing the need for a series of excuses, decided to tell the truth, or as much of the truth as seemed advisable. She explained that she hardly knew Bill, had been glad to help his daughters in their sudden trouble, but was not ready to be a stand-by for him or his family. "Why don't you invite Irma Beaton?" She felt a little twinge of guilt as she made the suggestion. What if Irma became interested in this sadly Catholic neighbor? Oh well, perhaps Irma would be willing to take a chance in return for some entertaining evenings. Anyway, she was old enough to decide for herself; so Polly repeated the suggestion and Millicent Morgan seemed to accept it, and hung up after a polite good-bye.

"Tomorrow everyone will know that I'm a selfish person, not ready to share a neighbor's sorrow," Polly thought ruefully. Never mind, better in the long run to have her defenses made clear to everyone. She dialed Frances's number. She would have to make sure Fran and Carl were free to go out for dinner, so she wouldn't be a proven liar. What a tangled web we weave! Luckily, Carl and Fran were free and glad to go out with her (though they preferred the Sand Bar to the Sea Food Shack, so there was a minor adjustment to the tangled web that was her excuse to Mrs. Morgan).

Dinner out would be fun: crab cakes or almond-crusted grouper, a change from home-cooked meals. Funny, people in Palm Haven all seemed to cook mid-western meals still when they ate at home: pork chops, roast chicken, stew. This was not a vegetarian generation. Meat and potatoes took precedence over green and leafy. In spite of living on the Gulf coast, the closest they came to sea-food was tuna casserole, made, as they would have made it at home, with canned tuna, mushroom soup, noodles, and a little green pepper. Residents from the New England States added salmon to their repertoire but even they were chary of trying to cook mahi-mahi. Most people had given up baking and making deserts and had taken with enthusiasm to Florida fruit, until an overdose of grapefruit left them with sore leg muscles. But when Palm Haven folk went out for dinner, they wanted clam chowder and crab cakes and Key lime pie, and a wonderful feeling of living in a new world, on the early bird specials.

Polly watched her budget and didn't eat out very often. The next big meal would no doubt be Thanksgiving, three weeks away.

The three weeks passed in the regular round of Coffee-Cuppers on Mondays, water exercise in the pool on Tuesday and Thursday, line dancing on Friday, church on Sunday, occasional fill-ins at bridge in the evenings. In local politics, Ginger Elrick had been nominated, had given a good speech at the candidates' meeting, had then been elected, and assigned to the redecorating committee; so the coffee hour had become dominated by talk about style, color, pizzazz, tone, image – to the point that Ginger's husband Jackson began to drop out of the gatherings, declaring he preferred to stay at home to read the paper, and catch up on some real news.

Polly drifted through the days, as she had done since moving to Florida. Lots of time to read, to walk around the lake, to get a haircut, to sit in the blessed sunshine, to drive to the beach to watch the incredible sunsets, to plant begonias ("Imagine planting flowers in November!"). The lake was filling with birds of all kinds, arriving from their long flight from the chilling north. Gulls floated gracefully, disturbed occasionally by the awkward arrival of pelicans flopping onto the waves and then flapping their wings into the fresh water, presumably to clean off the salt from the gulf.

One late afternoon she was doing a little weeding in her front garden when Bill pulled into his driveway, sat a few minutes in his car, and then came slowly across the grass to speak to her. "You're having a very busy social life," she said to him. His smile was not very enthusiastic.

"People are certainly being more than kind. I have led such a quiet life the last three years that I find it hard to be so sociable."

"You need time to yourself, to work your way through what has happened."

Bill smiled. He had more to say. "I wanted to tell you that I know you don't want to be involved in my doings right now. I've heard some rather slanted comments. I don't know if you realize? I thought perhaps you were offended at me somehow. Maybe you thought I had gone back too soon to my golf, and to all these dinner parties?"

Embarrassing. But it was important to explain, to clear the air. "It's nothing to do with you, Bill. I've always found it hard to be sociable myself." Something more was needed, some more reassurance. "I think it's wonderful, Bill, the way you've picked up on your old life. Your golf for instance. You're getting out, getting exercise, seeing your friends, keeping in shape."

"That's exactly how I feel," he said. "Especially the getting out part. The course is so great right now! A little mist in the early morning, then the sun coming out, everything green and sparkling, especially after that nice rain a few weeks ago."

How anyone could refer to a hurricane as a nice rain was hard to imagine, but the point was right. Everyone said the golf courses were in great shape this year, different from the drought last year when watering had to be limited and the fairways got very rough.

Polly repeated "I think that's wonderful," and picked up her trowel again. But Bill had more to say. "Well, at least I hope you won't mind if I ask you again about coming out for dinner with Lorraine and Loretta and me, maybe the Sunday after Thanksgiving Day? Every time the girls phone they remind me to ask you again."

There was no way to refuse.

Thanksgiving was approaching fast. Neither Tansy nor Hal would come down for the holiday – as expected. Polly would join Carl and Fran and their two sons, the daughters-in-law, and the collection of five grandchildren.

Carl was the cook in the family, and his two sons helped him prepare a special treat for the women and children, an old-fashioned feast: turkey, with chestnut dressing, mashed potatoes and gravy, green beans, yam and carrot casserole, cranberry sauce, pumpkin pie and ice cream; pink lemonade for the children, pretty pink Zinfandel for the grown-ups; jokes and laughter for everyone. "You're certainly off your diet today, Dad!" Norman Andersen laughed.

His mother cut in with a big smile, "Not just today! The doctor told him that his cholesterol was down, so he went out and bought a quart of cream!" Everyone roared with renewed laughter.

"Tradition!" Carl cried happily, in a final toast, and the dinner ended with a traditional family argument, furious, full-blast, affectionate.

When the young people had gone back to their motel, and Carl had collapsed in front of the television, Polly stayed to help do the dishes. "So easy nowadays with the blessed dishwasher," said Fran. "Remember the hours with the dishpan after big family get-togethers? Sometimes we would set up two separate dish-pan assembly lines, one in the sink, one on the kitchen table."

"And a tea towel in the dish-pan to protect the good china."

"And the silver and glasses done first, and then fresh water and detergents for the dishes, and again for the pots."

"And even earlier, before detergents, when we were little girls, chips of soap in a mesh cage, swished around in the water to make suds. You really had to rub hard when you were drying to get off the marks of the soap."

"You could tell a good dish-washer by the number of wet tea towels at the end."

They both sighed happily as the last dishes went into the dishwasher and the machine began to hum. "So what about Bill and company, Polly?"

"Well, the girls are here, Lorraine with her little girl and Loretta with her husband and nine-year-old boy. They are insisting on taking me out for a family dinner. Since I couldn't make it on Thanksgiving itself, they have made reservations for Sunday, at the Chart House on Longboat Key."

"Pretty fancy," Frances cried.

Fancy indeed! It was a different, luxurious world at the gulf-shore restaurant. The children had been left with Loretta's husband, so it was just Lorraine and Loretta, Bill and Polly climbing the wide stairs between bougainvillea blossoms, and then following a cheerful young maitre d' to a window-side table. The buffet was particularly splendid, with Thanksgiving decorations still in place and the bounty of Thanksgiving translated into extra lobsters, shrimp, crab salad, scallops, grouper – and never a turkey casserole in sight.

"Did you girls cook Thanksgiving dinner for your dad?" Polly asked. The answer was no, they had all gone to McDonald's "for the kids." Too tired from the trip down to bother with a big dinner. Besides, there was today's treat to look forward to, and more treats coming. The kids wanted to see the Mote Marine, the Sarasota Jungle Gardens, the works.

"The children have never been to Florida before. Our mother was too sick all the time to have them. They bothered her, from the time they were babies." Loretta laughed. "I guess we bothered her too, from the time *we* were babies."

Bill, looking flustered by this turn in the conversation, excused himself and wandered away in the direction of the men's room. The girls turned confidential, thrusting quick comments. "Daddy's had a hard time." "Our mother was never easy to live with." "We hope to see him happier now." "We trust you to see he enjoys his life now."

Misplaced trust, Polly thought, but she had no intention of arguing now. No intention of keeping a comforting eye on Bill in the future, either. Meantime, here was Bill returning to the table, and it was time for pecan pie and coffee and a slow conclusion to an excellent meal.

"We're here until Wednesday, so we'll see you again, between outings," Loretta said as they pulled at last into Bill's driveway. Polly went home and fell into an overfed sleep.

On Thursday, the day after a noisy confusing departure next door, Polly had a different call. Mrs. Morgan, phoning from across the road, said, "I see our neighbor has lost his Thanksgiving company. My own son and grandchildren have gone too. I've been thinking about you this holiday. I realize now that I was tactless to invite you over a while ago as a – a sort of –"

"A sort of set-up for Bill?" Polly laughed. Mrs. Morgan laughed in return. "I hadn't heard that term. But I guess that is what I meant. But now I would like to invite you yourself, just to come over and have lunch with me."

Polly gulped. She had lived here over four years, and this was the first friendly overture from the lady in the villa across the road.

The lady in question was continuing, with explanations. "I've lived here a very long time. I was one of the first people to buy here when the development first opened, you know. I used to be very much involved in all the activities. Gradually my friends either moved on to somewhere where there was assisted living, the Shores, or Westminster Towers, or somewhere like that, or else they – well, they died, you know."

Polly said, "I suppose that is what goes with living in a retirement community, Mrs. Morgan. We make friends, but we lose them too."

Mrs. Morgan corrected her. "Millie, please! I'm not that much your senior!" Then she went on, "I feel sorry now that I have been so unneighborly. I've watched you from across the road, but I've never called, except when I had that idea about giving Bill Magee a little company. I hope you will come over, just yourself, and the two of us can just have a little lunch together. Tomorrow, or the next day, or whatever suits you?"

Polly said, carefully, "Tomorrow would be fine, M –Millie. I'm not very busy. But," she felt she had to add, "but I'm as busy as I want to be."

"Fair enough," the older woman laughed. "You don't want to take on any regular visiting. Neither do I. I just want to make amends for being less than friendly – for a whole four years!" Polly suspected that she had found a fellow spirit. Surprising, considering that she had been judging old Mrs. Morgan as something of a gossip and busy-body, twitching the Venetian blinds in her front windows to keep tabs on the goings-on at Bill's place. Perhaps that had just been the shadowy aftermath of a former life as an active member of the community. Lunch next day would make a nice diversion, an unexpected easing down from the turbulence of Thanksgiving. Because there had been turbulence; not only the noisy comings and goings of Bill's grandchildren next door, but the emotional turbulence that stirred up each year in the absence of Tansy and Hal, the sense of a past life really finished. "I might as well settle down into being like Mrs. Morgan," Polly thought. "Mind my own business, twitch the Venetian blinds once in a while, make a very occasional neighborly gesture, and for the rest of the time, just watch the birds on the lake and enjoy the sunsets."

Millie Morgan had gone to quite an effort for her "little lunch": a cheese soufflé that had obediently risen to a fluffy height, a green salad with unusual vinaigrette dressing ("the secret ingredient is calamandine juice") and then fresh strawberries, Florida style, white at the heart, ruby red on the outside, and delicious all through. Accompanied by home-made ginger cookies. "I must admit I am exhausted," said the hostess. "I don't bake at all as a usual thing. I don't have dessert any more, either. But I've enjoyed myself this morning, getting ready for you!"

Polly couldn't resist a question, "What did you serve when you invited Bill over for dinner?"

"I must admit I bought a frozen lasagna at Publix. It turned out to be very tasty. And I had frozen yogurt for desert – no effort in that, either!" Millie rose to clear the table, and of course Polly carried her own dishes out to the neat red-and-white kitchen. Her hostess told her, "I did invite Irma Beaton that evening, as you suggested. Did you know that?" Polly rather sheepishly admitted that she had known about Irma's presence. She had done a little Venetian-blind twitching of her own on the evening of the visit.

Millie had another question or two. Why had Polly decided to retire to Palm Haven? Answer: friends from school days, Carl and Fran Andersen, had talked her into a visit. "We went to high school together in a small town near Indianapolis. After I married and moved to up-state New York we still kept in touch. When I talked about retiring, they convinced me to come here."

Another question: "Your husband had died before you moved down south?" Answer: Yes. (And no need whatsoever to explain that he had deserted her many years before he died. Neighborly chit-chat was one thing, baring the heart was quite different.)

Mrs. Morgan switched to a final, less personal question: How was Ginger Elrick doing with plans to redecorate the clubhouse? This answer came more easily. Ginger was promising something new and exciting, something stylish. That brought a sort of a "Humph!" from the older lady.

Polly and Millie parted on friendly terms, but without any definite plans to repeat the get-together. ("Though maybe at Christmas," Poly half-promised herself, "a return engagement, for politenes sake.

-5-   *SNOWBIRDS*

As Polly walked along the lakeside on Monday, an anhinga, the torpedo bird, suddenly surfaced near the shore. It seemed to keep pace with her for a while, gliding just below the surface of the water, its shiny head periscoping atop the sinuous neck. Then, as suddenly as it had appeared, it dived underwater, disappearing from sight. Polly walked on, waiting for the anhinga to surface again. Nothing. No disturbance of the shiny surface of the lake. Maybe it had circled back, in the opposite direction? Maybe it had made for a hiding place in the sedge at the water's edge? Strange bird, she thought. Strange encounter, somehow exciting and mysterious, though she had watched the ahingas many times, either in the water or drying their wings like miniature thunder birds, perched among the low branches of the Bottle-Brush tree.

Polly had been puzzled by another strange encounter this morning. Once again, Dr. Switzer had come over to stand in line beside her as she waited for her coffee. "Will you be at home at noon? I will phone you then, if convenient."

Once again she had said blankly, "Yes, fine," and spent the rest of the morning wondering what this second call would be about. Not another proposal for nursing help, surely. She could not have made herself more clear when he called the first time. "If I don't budge to help my best friend, I certainly won't budge to help that bossy doctor," she thought. The rest of the morning had followed its Monday routine: a short visit at Frances and Carl's house on the way home from Coffee-Cuppers, a phone call from Tansy, then a few minutes with the local paper before lunch time.

On the dot of noon, the phone call came. An abrupt opening: "Amy Malone is simply not able to help us in the clinic any more. Arthritis, you know. So I decided to give you another chance."

Indeed! Well, she had a ready answer this time, "There are three other nurses in the housing development. Former nurses, that is."

He countered that. "June Grant has already agreed to work with John Malone." He added, a little less firmly, a bit sheepishly in fact, "I have already asked the other two. They had already taken on other jobs."

Polly laughed and fell back on her second defense. "The truth is, I simply don't want to."

He was implacable. "Wants are not that simple. What you want, versus the wants of these underprivileged children, underfed, exposed to mistreatment, many of them, with undiagnosed diseases: they call it the well-baby clinic, but I've been there, and –"

"I'm sorry. But you'll have to find someone else."

"I'll tell you what. I will count on you for a week or so while I try to find a replacement. We need you from the fifteenth of December. You can surely come with me just for the first two weeks."

"I don't like masterful men," Polly told him. "and my answer is definitely no."

He was clearly taken aback. "Masterful?" He hung up.

One thing about Bill Magee, in contrast: he hadn't a domineering bone in his body. In the first week in December he asked Polly a couple of times whether she wouldn't come over and help him finish off the sympathy food, still crammed into his freezer, but he took her refusal with no apparent resentment. Polly wondered at intervals how he was managing with the unhappy job of sorting through Elnora's things. There were no visible signs of a big clean-out, only the perpetual green garbage bags, the row of them in the car-port steadily replenished, steadily put out on garbage day, two in Bill's can, two in hers.

"I should explain about the garbage," Bill said to Polly late one afternoon on his return from golf. "I'm gradually getting rid of the TV dinner plates." Then, to her puzzled expression he offered more explanation. "That's what I fixed for Elnora all the time: those ready-to-eat meals, Stouffers and so on. But we didn't throw out the plates, aluminum or plastic or whatever, just stacked them. Elnora's great motto was `waste not, want not', and she couldn't bear to think we were throwing out those plates. She thought they might come in handy some day. Now I know they won't, and I'm gradually getting rid of them."

To her question, "Wherever have you kept them, Bill?" he gave a careless answer, "Why, the spare-room cupboard is full of them. In garbage bags, of course, and washed before they were stored. Still, they do fill the cupboard. Even now I've just got rid of about half of them. And of course all the drawers in the spare room are full of Elnora's warm clothes, in case we ever went north again. They've been there for years. I guess that's my next job."

No wonder Elnora's daughters didn't relish staying in their parents' house, Polly thought. She couldn't help asking, "Will the girls be back at Christmas to help you?" and was not surprised at his answer,   "Oh, I couldn't expect them to do that kind of job. They have their own families, and Lorraine has a job, too – she's a teacher. Household science, you know."

Polly repressed a gasp. Good heavens!

Christmas was a little bit in everyone's minds now. Florida had its own way of previewing the season. Santa Claus arrived in Burdine's, in a very big white beard and very small red shorts. Angel banners appeared on the bridge that went across to Palmetto, and a few householders began to string Christmas twinklers along the fronds of the palm trees. But there was no snow, no icicles, no scarves and mitts, no cold carolers. One fine evening a brilliant parade along the canals brought boats festooned with bright Christmas lights, reflected on the dark water. Crews of Santa's elves and other celebrants glided by, singing Jingle Bells under the ropes of red and green. Next, on the lake in front of

Polly's villa some of the hardy men in the condo anchored a raft bearing a good-sized pine tree, not lit yet, but looming in readiness for the magic moment.

Every time Polly walked around the lake at dusk now, new reflections glimmered as the sunset dimmed, repeating on the water the bright glow of Christmas lights in the neighbors' lanais. On December the twelfth the switch in the club house was flipped, and the tall tree of brilliant lights shone out on the lake, its cone shape redoubled in blurred colors on the peaceful water. Christmas in Florida meant a festival of light.

The club house was resplendent with wreaths and candles and ribbons. "How can you hope to improve on the way it looks now?" Fran asked Ginger, who had now been elected chairman of the decorating committee. Ginger's answer was clear. The rooms looked nice, but everything was becoming a bit dowdy, with faded drapes, tired carpeting, and furniture in need of refurbishing. "Everyone will be pleased with something brighter and more in style," Ginger promised. The committee had come to an interim decision. They would depart from traditional Florida colors, and opt for richer, darker colors, oxblood red, olive green, and tan. "There's a man on the committee – Frank DiCaccio – " Ginger explained, "who used to be a designer, a decorator. He says these colors are totally in, up in New York. Frank says that even for Florida, there's no need for beige to dominate our spectrum."

. "How do the rest of the committee feel about that?" Carl asked.

"Oh, they don't say much. I guess they are as bowled over by Frank's ideas as I am. Of course everything is on hold right now, till Christmas is over."

Polly bought her air tickets, ready to fly to Buffalo to be at Tansy's over the holidays. Hal and his family would fly up from Raleigh for a couple of days too. It would have been easier, and cheaper, for the three units to get together in Raleigh at Hal's place, but Tansy wanted her children to spend Christmas up in the snow belt, and what Tansy wanted usually won out.

By December 15th the spirit of the holiday was really simmering. When the phone rang that morning, Polly assumed it was Hal, making sure her tickets were in order, and arranging to meet her next week in Buffalo. But no; it was Dr. Switzer, announcing – announcing! – that he would be picking her up this afternoon at 1:45, on the way to the clinic.

"*What?*"

"As arranged," he elaborated, not very patiently. "Surely you remember this is the day we begin our tour of duty?"

"Your tour of duty, maybe, Not mine! I told you I couldn't. Wouldn't."

"I assumed you were kidding." He forestalled her response. "At any rate it's too late now for these quibbles. I really need you. That is – the children and the mothers at the clinic must have a nurse, to work along with me." His voice became more propitiatory. "Come on, you'll enjoy the work once you get there. I know it's hard to pick up the threads again when you've been leading a life of – " He seemed not to have a way of finishing the sentence.

Polly knew the right word: "Self-indulgence." Even though she resented the implication, she could accept the justice of his attitude. Clearly, there was no way he could get along without her help at this late hour. She would have to go to the clinic with him.

She put on the cotton suit she had worn to the Magee funeral. Straight-cut, and dusty pink, not too remote from a uniform, it would not appear so clinical as to scare little children.

The clinic was in a rambling one-story building, with a crowded front yard, where mothers had parked their older children, to play on the swings and slides. Inside, it was vaccination day for the two-year-olds. There was no back entrance. The doctor and the nurse had to push through the group in the yard, then through the crying crowd in the waiting room, and then back to the doctor's small office, with its desk, examining table, chair for the mother, sink – and a minimum of free space for the nurse to work in. Vaccination day.

Polly had forgotten just how tired your back can be when you stand on your feet too long. And when you stoop to lift little children. And when you hold babies tightly enough for the doctor to give the vaccination. How tired your cheeks can be when you smile and smile and speak with assurance. "This is Melissa Mae, doctor. She's a very good little girl. You be nice to her now!" Then the "Waaagh!" of the small person, offended by discovering that the prick of the needle was not painless.

Back to the waiting-room: "Next, please!" and the whole performance to be repeated with Jo-Jo or Earlene or George. The pace was furious. Occasionally a mother would try to redirect the doctor's attention from the vaccinating needle to the problem of

Jo-jo's ear ache, but the response was curt and the glance at the ear cursory. "Tomorrow is general day. Dr. Malone will look at the ear." Back to the routine of swabbing, pinching, the needle, the brave sniff or the honest wail. A brief break in the sequence occurred when a glance at one little head revealed a general crawliness and brought quick directions to the mother, followed by "Write down these instructions" to Polly, and a swift scribble on a prescription pad. Then back to the "Next please!" routine.

At the end of the long, long afternoon the doctor said, "Bravo, nurse!" then amended it sheepishly to "I mean `bravo, Mrs. Taylor!'" Polly responded "It's just Polly, please, Dr. Switzer." In return, a mumbled, "You can call me Rusty, as Malone does," and a hasty amendment: "Except that in the clinic of course it is better to say `Doctor'."

"Of course," said Polly, as she collapsed onto the car seat.

The doctor delivered her to her house and then sped away to whatever kind of dinner awaited him. Bill, watering the hibiscus at his front door, saw her moving very slowly up the walk to her door. "You look – "

"Exhausted?" Polly supplied. "Beat? Completely done in? You're right!"

Bill's answer was an offer to massage the back of her neck. "That really used to help Elnora when she first began suffering from backaches."

Polly had a fleeting worry that if this was the beginning of backaches she was not eager to move on to the later stages. She thanked Bill sincerely, however, and told him she was not quite that bad.

"Bad enough to be willing for me to provide supper for you?" The answer was a weary yes. This time he brought a frozen casserole over to her house and put it into the microwave while she put up her feet and accepted a nice cold beer.

Bill was a good listener. By the time she had retold the story of her afternoon, she had eased into seeing it as funny, and pathetic, rather than as bothersome and frenetic. It was good to share it all. When supper was over and it was time to go home, Bill said, with an easy smile, "You know, this is the kind of thing my daughters are on about. They want me to have someone to chat with and laugh with. It needn't be any more than that, you know, Polly. I do think we could have good times together." He didn't repeat the offer to massage her tired muscles, but she had a feeling that she might well have accepted the comfort, if it had been offered again.

Frances phoned the next morning. "How did it go?"

Polly was barely awake and not at all mobile. "Awful," she said, and then added, honestly, "But sort of fun."

"You know I'll never forgive you for letting that man bamboozle you into doing something much more strenuous than the Meals-on-wheels thing that I invited you to do!"

"I know, I know! Bamboozled is the right word. I don't yet know how it happened. I was there at the clinic and in action before I had agreed to even think about it!"

"Well, at least it's only till you go north for Christmas. Does he understand that?"

No; Polly hadn't tried to explain to the doctor that she was leaving a week from today, December twenty-third. "I'll tell him tomorrow. I guess I really am committed to do one more day, but tomorrow is the end. I have to have time to pack next week. Then I'm away for eight days. He will surely be able to find someone else by then."

When Dr. Switzer picked her up on Thursday afternoon, Polly was up-front with an announcement. "This is my final day. I'm flying to Buffalo on Tuesday."

Dr. Switzer was unfazed. "That's perfectly all right," he said. "The clinic closes from that day for the Christmas holidays. Emergencies go to the Memorial; all the regular visits are suspended until the Monday after New Year's." He swept into an explanation of the work to be done today – ear, nose and throat checks, and treatment of minor ailments. "Mostly colds, of course, and nothing we can do about it, except hand out aspirins and advise bed rest. Not that anyone will take the advice. They'll be glad to accept the aspirins though. Ear infections are something else, of course. Have you ever worked on an ENT ward?"

Polly admitted that she had, although long ago, and the doctor regaled her with a little lecture on new treatments and medicines for ear-nose-throat problems until they drew up at the dusty yard of the clinic. She crossed her fingers as they entered the room full of sneezers and wheezers. Heaven help her if she carried a cold to Tansy's house! The little worry vanished as she swung into action, calling in the mother who had waited longest. Exact self-policing reigned in the waiting room; no one disputed the order of treatment. The response to "next please" was always swift and eager. Never a break between patients, never a pause for nurse or doctor. The hours sped by, as exhausting as on the previous clinic day, and as unbroken by the kind of chat and joking that had always taken the edge off duty hours in the old days in the hospital. Dr. Switzer was swift, purposeful, accomplishing a miracle of pacing, but he certainly didn't inject an iota of fun into the process.

At the end of the day, however, as they trudged out to his car, he offered a sop. "Time for a little release," he announced. "The Malones have invited us to come to their house for dinner. I hope you have no other engagement." Polly had been assuming that Bill might mop up her spirits again with a quiet supper, but nothing had been said, so she accepted the invitation. "But I'm such a mess!" She gestured to her rumpled dress.

His answer was, "Amy Malone was a nurse herself. She'll understand. Of course she's really crippled with arthritis now and not able to practice, but she certainly won't be affronted by the appearance of hard work."

That reference to hard work seemed to be all the thanks forthcoming for the tough afternoon.

Polly looked forward to meeting Amy Malone, who never went to the Coffee-Cuppers or other social gatherings, although others had spoken of her as a very nice person, a great reader, and a former member of the chorale.

John Malone was waiting at the door, welcoming them in, settling them into comfortable chairs in the lanai, bringing them drinks and appetizers and then helping Amy cross from the kitchen to join them. It was obviously a struggle for her to walk, but her manner could not have been more welcoming. "June Grant will be here any minute," she added. "We included her in the gathering because you know she has been helping John on the alternate days at the clinic. Good for all of you!" She chattered on, bringing in the kind of anecdotes that Polly had always enjoyed, the stories about mischances on the wards, of triumphs and miscues, "nurses' talk" as Polly had always thought of this kind of chat. When June came, the same tone carried on, the two men sitting back and letting them giggle, John Malone with an indulgent smile, Dr Switzer more sober, but still visibly relaxing under Amy's chaffing. John slipped out to the kitchen, clattering pans and then finishing up the table setting in the dining room, putting out dishes and silver ware, sauces, margarine, salt and pepper shakers in case anyone was not on a salt-free diet, and finally filling the water glasses. All the while he kept calling across to the lanai, first urging Amy to "tell the one about the anesthetist who stuttered," and next saying, "Rusty, you're in charge of the drinks you know; don't let Polly wait for a refill!" They all sat down to a good dinner, a happy quintet, relaxed by their host and hostess into the kind of easy banter that seemed to have the swing of old friendships.

June Grant offered to drive Polly home, since she was going to that end of the housing complex anyway. They left the trio of friends setting about doing the dishes – or rather they left Amy egging them on from her chair while the men did the mop-up, still joking and happy. June said, off-handedly, "It's so good to see the three of them together. They've had some tough times, but you'd never know it."

Polly refrained from asking about the tough times. None of her business, and she assumed that this would be the last time she would catch a glimpse of the trio, since her "tour of duty" was over now. She had had a good time, but she was glad to slip into the quiet of her own home, a little light-headed from the drinks, and more than a little exhausted from the afternoon's work. Tomorrow she would begin to organize clothes for the trip north; tomorrow she would take back her library books and get some new ones to take with her; tomorrow she would do a good cleaning job on the kitchen to leave it in dying order, as her mother used to say, before going on a trip; tomorrow . . . Polly slept.

-6-   *MIST RISING*

Christmas holidays over, Carl and Frances came to St. Petersburg airport to pick up Polly on her way home from Buffalo. "Did you spread colds to everyone, courtesy of the clinic?" Frances laughed, and was not surprised when Polly had to answer ruefully "Yes" before switching to "Anything happen in Palm Haven while I was away?"

She heard a second-hand version of the news circulating at Coffee-Cuppers earlier this morning, the main news being that Ginger Elrick was now totally absorbed in the decorating committee and that her husband was making cross noises about her preoccupation.

Carl and Frances had brought packages of sandwiches for lunch. "Just figured you'd be hungry, and not have anything to eat in the house," Fran said. They had kindly assumed that Polly would rather have the picnic lunch in her own home, rather than coming over to their place, and indeed it was total joy to be back in her own crowded lanai, happily eating egg sandwiches and watching the pelicans swoop and settle on the lake. "You two are all I need in my life, after an overdose of children!" she said. "I'm so exhausted by the high little voices –"

"And the energy! The endless, exhausting energy! I always go to bed for a few days after our grandchildren visit us. You remember after Thanksgiving, Carl?"

Carl agreed. "We had a very quiet Christmas here, Polly. Both our families went to the in-laws, the other grandparents. They both urged us to come, but we declined, very sorrowfully."

"*Very* sorrowfully," Fran laughed. "Especially since both families would be expanded by other sets of grandchildren, our daughters-in-law coming from big families themselves. How many sat down for Christmas at Tansy's, Polly?"

Polly answered "Too many. Fifteen, to be exact. I used to have that many myself when Tansy and Hal were children, and there were cousins and elderly aunts and all that to be included, just as there are now. Too many, now, for me at any rate." She munched a second sandwich contentedly. "It's Florida and retirement for me, and very grateful I am that I wound up here."

They had hardly left when the phone rang. "Welcome back," said Bill. "I saw you drive in with Carl and Fran."

"Weren't you playing golf today, Bill?" He answered that the foursome had had to cancel, so he had been at loose ends all day. "I wondered if I could bring over something for supper, so you wouldn't have to think about food on your first day back?"

Polly accepted. The thought of warming up a TV dinner in the microwave was not so bad, after the surfeit of rich and fancy foods in Buffalo. A restful afternoon, then a nice quiet supper, a TV show (Monday nights were always good) and the prospect of peace and quiet for the foreseeable future: everything looked wonderful.

Alas, the future turned out not to be foreseeable after all. At one-thirty the next day, Dr. Switzer's car pulled into her driveway, and the doctor rapped insistently on her door. "Aren't you ready?" he said, taking in her old slacks and sweat-shirt. He was pulling the same trick as before Christmas, she realized, crossly.

"No, I'm not ready," she said fiercely. "How could you assume that I would be? I'm not going to the clinic with you again. I told you that before Christmas. Don't tell me you thought I was kidding. You're not going to dragoon me into action again. Thank you, but no!"

The doctor said coldly, "I apologize if I misunderstood. I thought you did a fine job, and I assumed you would want to repeat." Now he looked puzzled rather than masterful. "Indeed, I'm sure we had agreed that I would pick you up today. I can't manage without a nurse you know. We can't let the children down, now can we?" Since his voice was sad rather than angry, it diminished her own anger.

"I guess not," she said. "There's no reason I couldn't go, just this one last time. But I want to be perfectly clear –"

"Of course, of course!"

Another pause. "Can you wait while I change?"

He cried, "No need! These people will not expect a crisp uniform. You look – "

"Ready for action?"

He said rather sheepishly, "I was going to say you look splendid. But of course you don't. You just look –"

"Appropriate?" They both laughed, and Polly climbed into his car, a little mollified, but still adamant in determination not to let this drag on. "This really is my last time, you know." He nodded agreement.

That evening, at the end of a grueling session at the clinic, there was no invitation from the Malones for a reviving dinner. Bill was hovering, however, when Polly stepped out of the car. She turned to say goodbye to Doctor Switzer, and to make sure that he understood it was goodbye, as far as the clinic work was concerned. He seemed to have got the message. "I do appreciate your help," he said. "Even if –"

"Even if it was grudging?" she asked, but he hastened to say, no, no, he meant even if she couldn't see fit to continue. "Don't worry about this Thursday," he added. (As if she would!) "Amy said that if all else failed she had a former colleague in Bradenton who would fill the gap until I can get a more permanent arrangement."

Polly lingered at the side of the car. "You mean Amy understood that I meant it when I said I was quitting? And you refused to understand?"

"That's right," he replied, not echoing either her smile or her light tone. "I didn't think you could resist the chance to be useful."

To that, she had no answer.

As the doctor's car disappeared, Bill emerged from the shadow of his carport. "I got a bottle of Zinfandel," he said, "just on the chance that you'd be ready for a drink before dinner." He hurried on, "It's Swiss steak, rice and carrots, all ready for the microwave!" He brandished an aluminum dish of TV dinner. At the end of this tiring day, it sounded more than welcome.

Polly woke up early the next morning, filled with resolve to put into action an idea that had come to her in the wee hours of the night. She would phone Millie Morgan, invite her to Sunday dinner, and be ready to insert a word then about her friendly companionship with Bill. She had planned a possible menu during the sleepless hours after midnight: skinless boneless chicken, rolled up and covered with mushroom soup, topped with almonds; green beans, rice (very good last night, but could be better if not frozen and re-cooked.) Then after dinner, she would talk about the meals Bill was bringing over, and explain the kind of friendship they both wanted. That should put rumors to rest. No: in reality she would be launching an alternative set of rumors; but at least there would be a let-up of speculation as to whether she and Bill were a "romantic item."

It was still too early to phone Millie. The temperature had dropped quite a bit during the night. The thermometer showed fifty-six degrees, cold enough that the people doing their early morning walk around the lake were bundled into fleece sweat suits and gloves. Some were even wearing ear-muffs, the mark of those who had been in Florida long enough that their blood had thinned and they felt the cold very easily. Some were power walking, but most were strolling quietly along the lake path, watching the mist rise from the water, enjoying the coming of winter sunshine. Even after four and a half years in Florida, it still seemed strange that there was no snow to go with the cold. Of course, everyone was now watching the weather channel on TV, gloating a little bit as stories of winter storms came through, and pictures of icicle-laden trees. Here most of the trees were still green. Of course, some leaves had been shed from the live oaks and the Tree of Gold now raised bare gnarled branches, but the shiny palms brazened out any coldness Florida could offer..

Polly turned back from the window and rinsed her coffee cup. Time to call Millie Morgan and set up the Sunday dinner invitation.

Then a nice quiet Wednesday: a trip to the mall to get the week's supplies, a longer drive to the library for a new batch of books, and a walk around the Bradenton waterfront while she was nearby. That would still leave time for a game of shuffleboard with Fran and Carl and Irma, when she got back to Palm Haven, late in the afternoon. If Bill offered to come over at supper time, fine. If not, equally fine. And surely tomorrow would not bring a surprise demand from the doctor.

Tomorrow – Thursday – could not have been more unruffled. No masterful arrival, no demand for assistance. No pressure. And no sense of guilt, Polly told herself. Nevertheless, she turned over in her mind another idea that had been fermenting. Late in the afternoon she strolled over to Fran's house. She would re-introduce the idea of Meals-on-Wheels, she had decided. It was true, she should be doing more than vegetating. Besides, that would give her a genuine excuse if there was ever any further talk about the well-baby clinic. She could only take on so much at a time. Even Meals-on-Wheels was more than she had promised herself! What price total retirement now?

"Great! Great!" was Fran's response. "I've been giving Carl a tough time, trying to coerce him into taking on the job with me. Let's phone now, and maybe offer to begin next week?" Polly, as usual, was a bit bothered by Fran's enthusiasm. But what was new? That was the way it had been, even in school days, Fran running full tilt at life, Polly dragging along a little way behind.

.She told Fran about her plan for Sunday, and decided on the spur of the moment to include her and Carl in the invitation.

Fran demurred. "I thought it was against your principles to invite anyone to your place for a meal? You were going to do any necessary entertaining at a restaurant."

Polly mumbled, "Yes. Well – " and Fran tactfully dropped that topic and accepted the invitation gracefully.

By Sunday, Polly had remembered why the anti-entertaining-at-home principle had been established. She was thoroughly nervous. Once upon a time she had entertained frequently and well. When you get out of a habit it's very hard to slip back into it. She hadn't realized what a mess her house was and how much she had to do to make it minimally presentable.

Sunday morning before church she set the table. It was a very cold January day: they would not be able to eat in the lanai. Just as well, since the lanai was even more crowded than the dining room. She hauled out the blue wash-and-dry, no-iron table cloth and flipped it onto the dining-room table. Then, on impulse, she dug into the bottom of the linen drawer and pulled out her Portuguese cloth. Delicately strewn with appliquéd flowers, it was the memento of her one and only trip abroad. Right after Tansy got married, Tansy's new mother-in-law had suggested that they travel to Europe together. It was an "If it's Tuesday it has to be Belgium" sort of trip, but at the end of it they had stayed on for two wonderful weeks in Portugal in a condo on the Algarve. The pretty table cloth was the souvenir of that happiness in Portugal. No use saving it forever though. "I might use it again sometime when Bill comes over. We don't have to eat at the kitchen table every time," she thought.

When the Sunday dinner was over and she was carrying a tray of decaff into the living room, Fran asked, as if on cue, "You've been entertaining Bill quite a bit, haven't you Polly?"

Polly answered with one eye taking in Millie Morgan's reaction, "Yes, we're having dinner together on Tuesdays and Thursdays. Maybe Sundays too sometimes."

Carl struck in, "He's a nice fellow, but he's very quiet. What do you talk about, Polly?"

The answer was honest. "We don't talk much at all. The weather, the letters to the editor in the morning paper sometimes. Mostly about Elnora, though. I think he needs to talk about her. Then we watch television for a while."

"Not very exciting," Carl said.

"No. I'm glad to do it, though, just until he gets through this first bad time and begins to build a life for himself again."

Millie had not contributed to this exchange, but she nodded. The point had been made: sharing evenings with Bill was a neighborly gesture, nothing more; but Polly suspected that the gossipy lady was saying to herself, "Nothing more – for the present, maybe."

Fran changed the subject. "Did you know that Polly and I are going to do Meals-on-Wheels, Mrs. Morgan?" The announcement evoked the inevitable "Call me Millie," and no other show of interest. Keeping an eye on the doings within the condominium was enough exercise for this elderly lady.

"What about the decorating committee?" she asked next. "Are they still set on a total change of style? That's what my friends tell me is in the air."

Carl had the answer: "We'll all hear their plans at the general meeting of the Condominium Association in February."

The party ended with friendly goodbyes from the guests and total exhaustion for the hostess.

Next day at Coffee-Cuppers, Irma and the younger couples were eager to hear how the Sunday party had gone. "Fine," she said bravely, and thought, "Oh dear. I'll have to invite them all to my house some of these days." She had been to a get-together at each of their houses and had trotted out her traditional spiel about never entertaining. "I've blown my cover now."

Irma switched the conversation. "I'm thinking of getting my eyes done."

"Cataracts?" Carl asked.

But no; Irma was thinking of having her eye-lids lifted. "You can hardly see my eyes, these days," she said. Polly noticed that Fran, like herself, had raised a tentative finger to touch an over-the-eye, drooping fold.

The main topic of the morning, however, was Ginger Elrick's progress with the decorating committee. They were almost ready to present their plans to the general meeting of the owners' association. "I hope you will all be there to support us," she smiled. "If you can round up extra votes among your friends, that would be dandy."

Her husband said, "Excuse me" and went back for a second cup of coffee. "Jackson finds me a bit boring right now, I'm afraid," Ginger said; but immediately went on with the campaign to find supporting votes. She turned to Polly. "How about Dr. Switzer – could you get him to back us up at the meeting?"

"Emphatically not," said Polly, and added, "He's not one of my friends anyway, Ginger."

"Just a working colleague?" Ginger laughed, having heard a wry version of the clinic experience.

As if to contradict that judgment, Dr. Switzer was seen approaching their table. Again, ominously it seemed, since it was a repeat of the earlier experience, he announced, "I will be phoning you after lunch. If convenient." Again, he stalked away before Polly could answer. Anyway, it was an announcement, not a question that called for an answer. Her friends made a game of thinking up all the excuses she could use if the doctor wanted to dragoon her into action at the clinic again. "Because there's no reason for any of us to do anything we don't feel like doing," Irma concluded. "We earned our retirement." There was a chorus of hearty agreement around the table.

In spite of the moral support, Polly picked up the phone after lunch with a little trepidation. Surprise – not a request on behalf of the clinic; something quite different. Dr. Switzer wanted Polly to go with him to the symphony in Sarasota on Friday night. John Malone, who usually went with him, had a touch of flu, and he hated to waste the ticket, since it was a particularly good program. "Charles Dutoit is conducting, and they're playing Mahler in the second half."

What could she say but "Thank you very much"? No doubt he saw this as a treat in return for her help at the clinic, and it *would* be a treat. Like many of her neighbors, Polly didn't often venture to drive into Sarasota at night. She could look forward to this trip with genuine pleasure.

She said as much to Bill Magee the next evening when he came over with dinner. Bill confessed that he had never been to the Van Wezel. Not much of a symphony fan. Elnora was not musical either, he said. He slid into the familiar focus on Elnora. "Such a pretty little thing. When she was young she was a great badminton player. In fact, she was in the state finals one year, and did very very well. Of course," his voice dropped from pride to melancholy, "she had to give all that up. First her knee went, after a bad fall. Then they did a knee operation, and that went badly, left her with a permanent list to the side. Then in turn her back was affected, and that meant another operation." He pulled up. "I've told you all this before, Polly."

"It must help you to go over it out loud, though, Bill, instead of just remembering in your private thoughts."

"Actually," he said, "I remember her more when I'm talking to you than when I'm alone. I guess I'm not the sort to have many private thoughts. I just totter on in my own way."

"Talking is good, though," Polly repeated, although she knew she could never tell anyone the story of her own life with Harold the way Bill was recounting his years with Elnora.

She put frozen yogurt into glass dishes and then realized that she had forgotten about putting the Portuguese cloth on the dining-room table. Never mind. Bill was more at home in the kitchen. He had mentioned that in all the years they had been in

Florida, he and Elnora had never used the dining room. It had been easier to bring a tray to her where she lay on the sofa.

"However did you manage before you came to Florida, Bill? I mean, when the girls were young."

"When Elnora was first laid up with the knee trouble we sent them to a convent school. A boarding school, you know. Then in the summers I got a caregiver to come stay with Elnora and I took the girls camping. We had fun."

"Not fun for me!" Polly laughed. "Camping was a total disaster as far as I was concerned. I tried it with Hal and Tansy, but it rained and was windy and generally miserable."

Bill regaled her with happier stories, of camping coast to coast with his daughters, getting back to Ohio just before school opened again. No wonder Lorraine and Loretta seemed to have few happy memories of their mother, Polly thought. Bill seemed perfectly satisfied with the family life as he remembered it, however.

-7- CONCERT

When Friday evening rolled around, Polly stood outside her villa waiting for Dr. Switzer to pick her up. On time, of course; in fact a few minutes before the time he had set, typical of Florida retirees, always ready before they needed to be. Polly was smiling at the thought as she got into the doctor's car, smiling again as she saw the flick of the Venetian blind across the street. Millie Morgan must be surprised at the livening of Polly's social life!

They traveled pretty well in silence to Sarasota, parked conveniently close to the Van Wezel. Going into the great purple blimp of a theatre was always exciting, and the program looked good. Good, but surely not good enough to create the intensity, the almost shaky excitement in Dr. S. as they climbed the wide stairs. He explained as they pushed along the row to central seats that the main offering was Mahler's fourth symphony, "The one that ends with the child's poignant song. I always find it very moving."

The concert clashed to an exciting opening with a Strauss polka, then modulated into one of Dutoit's French specialties, a delicate group of short pieces by Fauré.

Then came the intermission, and on their return, the Mahler symphony. As the opening movement grew from quiet chords into a blend of folksongs, rollicking sleigh-ride sounds and the stirring call of the trumpets, Polly could feel that her escort was growing excited, not exactly tapping his toes but moving his shoulders in a kind of surging sympathy to the succession of rhythms. The final movement began. A slim, beautiful young Afro-American soprano moved to center stage. As the movement unfolded, her voice, lyric, childlike, pure, lifted up, up; then gently ran down scales to come to a final gentle, consolatory ending.

Dr. Switzer was so moved, apparently, that he didn't join the rest of the audience when at the finale they rose to their feet. Well, Polly thought, perhaps he felt, as she herself had sometimes felt, that this Van Wezel audience was too ready with its standing ovation, too indiscriminate to distinguish the really shattering performances from the competent ones. A glance at Dr. Switzer told her that such a critical thought was not what held him in his seat. He was dabbing his eyes with a carefully folded handkerchief.

The applause continued, swelled, and finally died. People began to push past them, moving toward the doors, and only then did he turn to her with a diffident smile. "It's the child's song that affects me in this ridiculous way. This symphony is one of my favorite CD's; I play it too much, I guess. To hear it this way, in this beautiful voice – it's too much for me."

He rose at last, and they joined the audience streaming to the side aisles. Out under the palm trees and the stars, moving to the car parked where it faced the dark bay, they stood in quiet for a moment. Maybe he'll tell me sometime why this one piece had such power over him, Polly thought. Or maybe not

"Sometime" came on the way home, as they drove along the quiet streets on the way to the condominium estate.

"You know that song at the end of the Mahler symphony is the song of a little girl. She is going to die, but she sings with such love of life! It moves me so terribly."

Polly sat silently, wondering if perhaps he had lost a daughter and whether that was the secret spring of his emotion.

As if he had heard her unspoken question, he explained. No, he hadn't lost a daughter. But in a sense he had lost all the children that once were the center of his life. "Pediatricians often seem callous to parents, I guess. Most are like I was, so centered in the lives of my patients, and so satisfied when I was working with children. The little girls, usually so good, so much easier to treat than rambunctious boys – rambunctious even when they're pretty miserable, you know!"

"Yes," said Polly, "I do know. I worked on the pediatric wards for several years when I was first nursing. The little boys were touching, they were so fierce in keeping up appearances, not admitting they hurt. I had my own babies then, and dealing with suffering in the little children, both boys and girls, turned out to be too much for me. I shifted to other wards." There was a little silence. "You didn't shift, of course," she said to the doctor. "You just went on enduring."

"Oh, yes," he cut in, "and enjoying, of course! All the funny things the little patients say and do. There was one little guy –" He launched into an anecdote, apparently happy to shift from his earlier mood, and ready to cover his pathos with a wry smile.

And then when they were safely on the road home, he reverted to his distress. "I often feel now that I failed so many of them. Too busy to go all the way in concern, and too absorbed in my own children at home to give the patients the extra inch of attention that might have made a difference. Then, my own children: I eventually felt I had short-changed them too, because of being as absorbed as I was in the practice. So I lost both ways. I could never do enough for any of the children, my own or my patients."

"You're human," Polly said. "There's only so much anyone can do."

He made no answer. By the time they pulled into her driveway, his face had set again into its lines of cold control. She thanked him for letting her hear "such glorious music." He simply answered, "Good night."

Next morning it was raining, for a change. After a cold January (so cold it had nipped Polly's begonias), the February weather had been an unbroken succession of sunny pleasant days and gradually warming weather. Last night there had been a spatter of raindrops on the skylight in the kitchen, and a roll of occasional thunder.

Now it was pouring, a tropical power storm. Polly wandered around the house, feeling vaguely disquieted. Probably a reaction to change in itself, she thought. She was becoming very adverse to shifts in regular routines, including shifts in the weather. She had become so settled into this villa life over the past four years; so relieved to be out of the swing of things. She remembered a fragment of poetry from school days: "calm of mind, all passion spent," and said it over to herself with relish. She had had enough of disruptions in her earlier life. Now she seemed to become depressed and disturbed by changes.

Pacing around her little domain, she reconsidered the events of the past few months, especially the increasing encroachment into her days of Bill next door, with his recurring presence at supper time. Dr. Switzer had been an even more disrupting presence, all the more disturbing because there was no semblance of regularity or peacefulness in his intrusions. The rain poured down, flooding her little garden, beating an irregular tattoo on her windows, waves of sound, growing and receding.

Community life went on, with its own rhythms and tides. Ginger Elrick was bubbling with energy and enthusiasm when she settled into the coffee group on Monday. "Our committee is really going full steam," she confided. Frank says we've been in a box, thinking that Florida colors had to be shell-pink and foam-green."

"Tell me again – who is Frank?" Carl asked.

"Frank DiCaccio."

"Don't know his name."

"Frank's a newcomer – bought his place here at the same time as the Vanderburgs and ourselves."

"And he was elected to the committee too? They usually manage to put on only one newcomer at a time."

"Well, actually, he wasn't elected. I co-opted him. I'd heard about him from a friend of mine in Venice, who used him when she was building her new house. It's gorgeous –"

"I just wondered," said Carl. "I heard some rumblings when I was playing billiards on Friday. Some of your committee seem a bit dubious about him."

"Well, they don't bring up any questions at the committee meetings, so I have to assume they are in essential agreement with our ideas."

"Probably so." Carl let the matter drop and the rest of the group turned to talk about Irma, now out of circulation for a little while, after her small cosmetic operation.

Back home at Fran and Carl's, Carl reverted to his little worry about Ginger's committee. "There is a clique of older residents who tend to gang up against anyone new, even while bemoaning the fact that none of the younger people are putting as much into the condominium as the older ones did in their day."

"We'll be the same, pretty soon, Carl," Frances said. "I'm already beginning to resent the little changes that have crept into the development since we've been here."

"'Change and decay in all around I see,'" Polly quoted with a smile.

Fran reacted in mock horror. "Don't talk about decay, please!" She lifted her hands as if to hide the fine wrinkles webbing her pretty face. Carl reached over, took her hand, and kissed it.

"Time for me to leave, you two!" Polly was laughing as she moved to the door of the lanai and stepped out.

When she reached home, she found Ginger Elrick waiting for her, sitting on the deck chair outside the lanai door. She had come for a little advice on the politics of Palm Haven. "Because I'm running into a lot of puzzles, things everyone else seems to understand."

"Like what?"

"Everywhere I go people have been buttonholing me and criticizing what they hear about our ideas. Everything the committee has discussed, colors, styles, borders, costs, everything, is a matter for furious argument. Half the time I don't know what the disagreements are all about."

"Poor you! But at least you hadn't any built-in agenda," said Polly, "no fixed ideas left over from previous battles about décor –
"

Ginger capped her comments, "And not a clue about why some people feel so desperately strongly about tiny little things. Every day for the past two weeks someone has phoned to tell me what they think about our plans. How they know about them is beyond me. Someone on my committee must be dribbling bits of information."

"It's not supposed to be a confidential committee is it, though?"

"No. But Frank has emphasized all along the value of surprise and urged us all to keep the plans to ourselves. Obviously, some people can't cooperate. The reaction to the leaks of information is incredibly strong."

Polly had her own theories about the source of the strong feelings. Maybe it was just that there was so little else to occupy the minds, the strong, used-to-decision minds of the people who had retired here. Maybe it was a hangover from the desire to make one's habitation perfect, even if now it was a shared habitation, a clubhouse in a condominium, not a apartment or house or cottage privately owned and open for individual expression of taste. Maybe it was an afterglow of power drive, which had been strong enough in all these people to have left them in a position to afford a moderately expensive condo life.

No point trying to explain all this, Polly thought, and she simply said, "I'm not a good resource on politics. I've been here four years without understanding how things work. But I'll take you over to meet Millie Morgan, across the road. She knows everything that ever happened here; every secret undercurrent, who's opposed to whom, and why; what the hot issues are and why."

Ginger laughed too and agreed that she should visit Millie.

"We have to give her fair warning, though," Polly cautioned. "We can't just barge in. She's a formal lady. Once she thaws a bit, she'll clue you in on all the do's and don'ts."

"Just what I need," Ginger said. "You know, Polly, I'm a political animal. I've always liked being on the inside, keeping things working."

"Not me!" Polly interjected. Then curiosity drove her to a question, "Is your husband the same? Politically minded I mean?" Everyone knew that the Elricks were virtually newly-weds, married just before they moved into Palm Haven last spring. Jackson Elrick was a quiet man, not contributing much to Coffee-Cuppers conversations on Monday mornings; but of course there was usually so much buzz of conversation that perhaps he had all kinds of opinions as yet unexpressed.

Ginger satisfied her curiosity. "We're quite unalike, I suppose," she said. "We agreed when we moved down here that we should each find our own way in this new life." With a little hesitation, she picked her next phrases carefully. "We each went through an ugly divorce, in order to be with each other. We had to work out in advance how we would – "

"Co-ordinate your new lives?" Polly suggested, and Ginger grinned and agreed.

"Exactly. I hesitated about letting my name stand for the steering committee, for fear Jackson would think I was neglecting him. Then I realized that if I were here alone I would certainly have wanted to run for office, so I just went ahead. Jackson is joining an investment group, which doesn't interest me. I expect we would be going our separate ways exactly like this if we had been living together for years. I'm glad he agrees that I have my own life to live, in my own way."

"Lucky you!"

"I gather you've been through a divorce too, Polly, so you know how hard it is to regain self-esteem. How easy it is to be very defensive after you finally find yourself on your own again."

Polly just smiled. Just as she had not invited Ginger in to her house, she was not about to tell her about her own long-ago divorce, or her own hard-won (and still only partial) self-esteem. But she was glad to hear Ginger's story and glad that her new friend was working out such a sensible basis for her new relationship. She switched the conversation back to the need to phone Mrs. Morgan to arrange for Ginger to visit the condo oracle.

"Fine by me," said Ginger, and she moved away, jaunty and self-confident, in spite of her set-backs.

Certainly, Polly thought, after Ginger had left and before Bill arrived with his customary TV dinner, certainly, if self-esteem in a woman depended on having a man invite her out occasionally, she was experiencing a decided rise. Dr. Switzer had phoned again, to ask if she was free on Saturday to join him. This time the invitation had been to go together to a championship tennis match at Meadowbrook. She had told him frankly that she was not interested in tennis. After a shocked silence he had explained. This was a State semi-final tournament. Some of the players would probably emerge some day as world champions. It had happened before. Florida was a famous training-ground for champions. . . .

Polly had heard him out and then repeated that she just didn't find tennis very interesting to watch. She had tried once to watch the Wimbledon series on TV and found that boring. So, thank you very much, but – . She knew he considered she was making a mistake, but she just couldn't face hours of sitting watching a game that held no interest for her. "Please don't turn up on Saturday with the idea that when I declined your invitation I was 'just kidding'."

With a little snort of laughter and a formal "Goodbye then," he had hung up the phone.

She was smiling a little at the memory, whether in enlarged self-esteem or a tickled sense of the ridiculous, when Bill Magee knocked on her door, laden with dishes of dinner to be microwaved and a bottle of California Chardonnay as a starter. "I was telling Loretta about our dinners together and she suggested that a little wine would add a nice touch," he said, ingenuously.

A further boost to self-esteem? Or a reminder to keep self-defenses in better array? She had brought out the embroidered Portuguese table cloth earlier this afternoon; now she whisked it away and set two informal places at the kitchen table.

From Ginger, a few days later, she heard about a very different get-together. Mrs. Morgan had been delighted to lunch with Ginger, and even more delighted to give her advice on how to run her committee's affairs. "She says the essential thing is to involve everyone early on," Ginger recounted. "She thinks that before the general meeting, we should call an interim sort of Town Hall meeting or round-table, where everyone can vent their ideas. Then we should incorporate a few of those ideas into our plan."

"And is that what you will do?"

"Maybe. I'll see what Frank DiCaccio says. "

But Frank, as Ginger reported by phone the next evening, disagreed. "Frank says clients are usually ready to take the experts' advice. You can't put together a decorating scheme out of little patches of individual ideas. You need a firm master plan. Frank says if we open up the discussion now, they will all want to go back to the pale wishy-washy colors. But when they see the total design, the swatches of materials, the mockup of changes, they'll be bowled over."

"I can't imagine Millie and her friends being bowled over that easily."

"No. But the older people are not in the majority any more. They'll just have to join the world."

Polly had done her own world-joining. This week, the Meals-On-Wheels idea had been put into action. Frances did indeed do the driving, but Polly was the one to organize and deliver the covered trays. Once the two of them had gone into a client's home together, because they had been warned that there was an extra need for help with feeding one old gentleman. They had slipped back to the car together, afterwards, out of the stifling trailers, and the sterile condos, unable to voice the pity and revulsion they felt. Joining the world was not easy.

All week Polly had found it hard to eat dinner after arriving home from these outings. She had to spend half an hour in her pretty garden, pulling up the odd weed, watering the new impatiens plants that replaced the begonias frost-touched in January, before she could face the supper hour.

Nevertheless, she was sleeping well, better than for a long time, and waking refreshed. In the winter mornings, stepping out from the lanai brought the pretty sight of mist rising over the lake. Near the lanai door a mallard duck slept, his beautiful iridescent head turned backward to nestle into his feathers. "Gathering strength for the mating season," Polly thought with a smile, remembering the frenzy of pursuit and flight among all the birds that would begin soon.

The human community seemed to be gathering strength, too. On Monday, Ginger arrived in a mood of excitement. "Frank has collected samples of materials, paint chips, and all that, and he has found good contractors to do the work. We're ready to put the whole plan before the Association, all worked out in exact detail, ready for instant action." She took another breath. "We're not going to bother with an interim plan. We will just cut right to the final decision, get it ratified week after next, and by summer the new look will be *fait accompli*."

"What about Millie Morgan's advice?" Polly asked.

Ginger said airily, "Of course we'll be open for minor suggestions and modifications. But since we were deputed to do the job of redecorating, we don't really expect many major suggestions. Millie is a dear, but you know she sees cabals and conspiracies everywhere. Things have changed since her day."

Something else had changed, too. Irma, rejoining the group at Coffee-Cuppers, caught a flutter of compliments as she opened wide her pretty blue eyes. The little operation had indeed enhanced her appearance. "And hardly any pain at all."

-8-   *ALLIGATOR*

Next week, Polly slipped in late to Coffee-Cuppers, to find a hot discussion going full blast. Ginger Elrick was speaking. "Seven alligators were found in this lake."

Instant reaction: "Surely not!" "In *our* lake?" "Who says so?"

"Mrs. Morgan says so." Ginger was quoting the keeper of local legends. "Well, not in the lake exactly. In the swamp that was here originally. When they dredged the swamp, they pulled out seven alligators."

"Never!" The group of friends looked out the clubhouse windows to contemplate the sunlit lake. They found it hard to believe that this shining expanse, with its manicured shoreline, had once been a mangrove swamp.

Alligators were in the news today. The morning paper had told of a woman, out for an early morning walk, who had disturbed a sleeping alligator, and been pulled into the river in a nearby park. Alligator stories had bubbled throughout the coffee hour. A poodle had been snatched off a leash. A baby had been pulled from a playpen set up too close to the water. Another woman had an arm crunched off before she had been rescued. Polly, who had taken her grandchildren when they were young to the Sarasota Jungle Gardens to see the alligator man wrestle with a baby alligator, remembered his dire warnings. She remembered also taking them when they were older to the Mayakka Park, to coast in a fragile boat along an alligator-laden river.

"I had alligator shoes when I was marr – when I was young," Irma remarked. The others, who had all heard the stories of Irma's trousseau many times, chuckled inwardly at her dexterity in deleting the reference to her first marriage. Bill had joined the coffee-cuppers group this morning.

"I always longed for a pair of alligator shoes," Polly admitted. Young (or rather youngish) Irene Vanderburg cried, "Ugh! That's as bad as wearing a fur coat!"

The older women burst into defense: "I had a sheared beaver." "Otter was the most expensive, but so silky." "There was no such thing as a down coat then. Up in northern Michigan we all had to wear fur in winter time."

Then, because today was an alligator day, the talk swung back. "Florida isn't just hibiscuses and peace lilies," Ginger said. "We have to accept the alligators." She sighed.

"Okay, dears," Fran said, "coffee is over. Time for the general meeting of the Association. They're setting up the chairs already."

The human alligators were waiting. Before Ginger was well launched into her display of modern designs and rich dark materials, the opposition began to be felt. "Looks like a funeral parlor!" someone interjected. "Looks like Wisconsin!" another voice growled, and the murmur of protests swelled. Peace was temporarily restored when Dr. Malone rose to suggest that the matter be sent back to the committee, with their deadline extended for a couple of weeks, so that they could receive suggestions in writing, and evolve a modified plan. Carl Andersen quickly seconded the motion.

Ginger unfortunately protested that postponement would be impossible, since the contractors had already been contacted and tied to an early date to begin work. The growls became an uproar.

"Tell them they will just have to wait," said the Association President; but Ginger, after a whispered conference with Frank DiCaccio, confessed that there was a deposit at stake, with a solid date written into it. That was the last straw. The meeting erupted; the President broke it up by calling the question on John Malone's motion, and the resulting vote left Ginger to cope with the necessity of getting the contractors to extend their deadline. In March, at the next General Meeting, the whole question would be opened again.

Fran had some practical advice for a furious Ginger. "Better see Millie Morgan again. She has every past battle stored in her memory. She may know the right way to win the next one."

Polly, reluctantly, offered to host another little lunch party. Ginger refused. "She's my hope, my possible life-saver on this whole mess. I'd better entertain her myself."

With relief, Polly agreed.

The next day's luncheon with Millie, according to Ginger, was no laughing affair. When it was over, Ginger phoned Polly to rehash the party and discuss Millie and her innuendos. "How can anyone keep so many old feuds and conspiracies in her mind? How can she continue to live here when she seems to see the place as a nest of innuendos?" She interrupted herself. "Can there be a nest of innuendos? I can't even put together an unmixed metaphor!"

"Come on," Polly laughed. "It's not that bad!" Then she realized she had never had a full-blast session on the topic of Palm Haven politics with Mrs. Morgan. Maybe Ginger was not exaggerating.

"You don't know how bad it was!" Ginger retorted. "Millie had been storing up all kinds of ideas since our last encounter. She is prepared to talk to her friends and twist a few arms, if I am prepared to moderate my views. After we agreed on that, she dished out all sorts of gossip about the committee members during the first course. But then –"

"Then what?" Polly could see Ginger was hesitant to continue. But continue she did: "Then she turned her guns on you, Polly, during dessert. She leaned up so close we were almost nose to nose and began, 'What's this I hear about our friend Polly Taylor and Dr. Switzer? Is she two-timing poor Bill? They say – "

"Don't tell me! Polly interrupted. "I don't want to know what they say!"

"Just as well!" Ginger laughed. Then, more seriously, "I was fuming. I shut her up as well as I could. Not very diplomatically I'm afraid."

"Anyway," Polly said.

Ginger picked up the word. "Anyway. Let's go out for dinner tonight, you and Jackson and I. I've got to get away. Off the campus, Jackson calls it, when we take off for Sarasota."

"I call it leaving the A.W.," Polly countered.

"The what?"

"The Ambulatory Ward. There used to be one big ward in every hospital, where people recovering from an operation could linger on, getting therapy, clinging to the security of the hospital. All indulging themselves a little."

"That wouldn't happen today," Ginger laughed. "They turf you out of the hospital the second you leave the operating table."

"Right. But in the old days we kept them in cotton wool for a while. They were happy to be over the operation, nervous about returning to the real world, content to stay forever in the A.W."

"Like most of the people in Palm Haven."

"Not like most; just a few. They're the ones that drive you to

—"

"To the need of a trip off campus. So how about tonight?"

Polly already had an engagement for that evening, however. "My brother is here," Bill had said on the phone in mid-afternoon. "We want to take you out for dinner, just for a change."

Bill's brother Bob was not just a brother, he was a twin. Sitting between the two of them at the Beach House Restaurant, Polly felt as though she was chatting with Tweedledum and Tweedledee. She had seen a resemblance on the day of the funeral, but had been too busy with other concerns to really look the brother over. And certainly she had not had a conversation with him then. Now, Bill and Bob, full blast, interrupting each other, laughing the same kind of laugh, turning toward her with the same little duck of the head, made a comic pair. Clearly, Bill and Bob knew what effect they had.

At the end of a laughing session, Bob turned serious for a moment. "You're sure good for this old guy, Polly. He hasn't been as much fun for years. My share in the improvement is that I made him promise not to mention Elnora once while we were out. It worked, didn't it Bill? You've had a right good time tonight."

Bill rather sheepishly agreed, and admitted that it was a relief to get his mind onto a different path. "I'll try to stay cheerful, Bob. At least till you come again to check on me."

"Don't dwell on the past. Stop memorializing Elnora."

"Agreed," Bill said. So there would be no Elnoralizing for a while, and Polly had to admit a sense of relief.'

February had ended. March Break would come early this year, and dinners with Bill, like Meals-on-Wheels, had to be put on hold, in anticipation of the imminent deluge of grandchildren during the annual school break up north.

Hal's girls, Miriam and Jill, arrived at the Tampa airport, traveling alone. In past years they had come with their mother. Now they were old enough to come alone, eager to join the flood of teenagers celebrating March with the new rites of spring, strolling the beach, hunching over pizza slices in the shade of the Australia pines at Coquina Beach, striking up conversations with other young teens, who looked as strange to Polly as did her own granddaughters. Jill and Miriam had been transformed since Christmas. Hair in orange spikes, in the one case, sleeked into a shiny black cap, in the other (equally startling to the eyes of a grandmother who had loved the gentle brown curls of so short a time ago.) Obviously, though, they looked perfectly ordinary and acceptable to the eyes of their contemporaries.

Next door, Bill's grandchildren arrived with their mothers and went off to the Sarasota Jungle Gardens, the miniature golf, the Mote Marine, the Bradenton manatee museum, all the places Polly had taken her own grandchildren when they were a bit younger. Lorraine and Loretta and their respective spouses and offspring were staying at the Holiday Inn nearby but coming every day to sweep Bill away on their expeditions. Bill had tacitly suspended his dinner presentations while the young people were in evidence. Every evening, however, Lorraine or Loretta called over to Polly, inviting her and the young Taylors to come out together for a fast food binge. Polly ran out of excuses for refusing to join forces with the Magee circle, and she had to admit that her granddaughters seemed to enjoy the outings together, to Capalbo's for Pizza, to the Athens for gyros, to the Burger King for hamburgers.

As the week progressed, it became customary for the two families to merge at suppertime, to everyone's apparent pleasure. It was the time of day when all the teenage boys and girls seemed to disappear into their own families. Jill and Miriam seemed content to blend in with their grandmother's neighbors, even though these were just "little kids".

On Friday, startled, Polly overheard the youngest of Loretta's children say to Miriam, "Wouldn't it be fun if your grandma married my grandpa?"

Miriam looked startled too. Obviously she had not thought of her grandmother as marriageable.

Later, remembering the overheard conversation when she was in bed that night, Polly added alarm to her own startlement. What had the children heard? Were Bill's girls conspiring to push him into marrying again? So soon? And why? Maybe they wanted someone to relieve them of having to listen to what she thought of as Bill's "Elnoralizing", the constant recalling of their mother's charms? Maybe (her thoughts became even less charitable), they thought this would be a way of avoiding having to clear up his house and disposing of their mother's belongings?

Loretta dispelled some of the uncharitable thoughts the next day. She dropped over for a chat while the children were having a final visit with their grandfather before they all drove away back North. "We do so want Daddy to have a little happiness," she said. "We think he had a rotten life for the last thirty years at least. Both

Lorraine and I appreciate your kindness in spending so much time with him."

"Only Tuesdays and Thursdays for supper," Polly demurred in some alarm. "Sometimes on Sundays. Just as a neighborly gesture. "

"Sure," Loretta said quickly. "We don't want either of you to feel rushed. It just seems so great that you're here, while we're so far away. And that you're so – so congenial."

"Not that congenial," Polly said firmly. "I don't mind chatting with your father and watching TV with him, but I have my own life. I'm here for myself, not for anyone else. You'll have to understand that, Loretta. I suspect there's a bit of a conspiracy gathering here between you and Lorraine. I just want you to know that I'm happy as I am, and I don't mean to change."

"Sure, sure," Loretta said again. She stood up, pushed a fall of long hair behind one ear, and made a hasty getaway before Polly could protest any more.

Polly thought she had better say something to her own granddaughters before she took them to the plane on Sunday evening, to forestall any false rumors spreading to their father in Raleigh, and beyond Hal to Tansy in Buffalo. Somehow she couldn't find any way of broaching the subject to the girls. They had a happy final day at the beach, in perfect March weather, with a perfect array of boys and girls their own ages, all promising faithfully to keep up the spring break friendships, by email, when they got home. Their thanks for the holiday were genuine and boisterous, very different from the polite "thank you" of earlier years when they had come to Florida accompanied by their mother. No credit to me, Polly thought, just a reflection of the girls' luck in arriving at this stage of life without illness or homeliness to impede their sociability.

After Coffee-Cuppers (very quiet, a reflection of grandparental exhaustion), Polly drifted home from Fran and Carl's to find messages blinking from the answering machine, and the phone itself ringing. Tansy. Oh, dear. Tansy, full of the news from Hal, and the opinion that Polly was letting herself in for big trouble by encouraging "that Bill." Tansy's voice was taut with tension: "So what's going on, Mother?"

"Nothing. We just have dinner together occasionally."

"I hear it's three times a week."

"Yes, well, it's just for now, to ease Bill back into life post-Elnora."

"You're letting those terrible girls unload their responsibilities on you."

"That may be what they're after, all right. But I'm not taking over Bill's life for them."

"You will be, if you let him become a habit with you."

"Not a problem, really, Tansy. In fact –" Polly scrambled for a defense against her daughter's concern –"in fact I'm going out with another man these days." (Let me be forgiven, she thought, for labeling one evening of music and one rejected invitation to a tennis match "going out with.")

This was a new challenge for Tansy. "Another man? Who?"

"Well, actually it's the doctor that I worked with at that clinic. Before Christmas. I told you about it, you remember."

"Yes, but you found him a holy terror! Masterful, you said, and I know that is your pet word for someone you don't like."

"Well, he's masterful, all right. I'm taming him down." As she spoke Polly knew she was getting into deeper waters with Tansy, who had always been like a pup at a root when she got an idea into her head. "Anyway, Tansy, don't get excited again. I just meant to ease your mind about Bill."

Recalled to her original alarm, Tansy delivered strong advice against both Bill and the masterful man. "Not that I mean to try to run your life, Mother. If you're having fun, that's wonderful. It was just Hal's call that alarmed me. Jill and Miriam – "

"They have typical teenage love of exaggeration."

"Of course. Yes." Tansy's voice returned to its normal level. "And everything else is going along okay? Meals-on-Wheels?"

So Polly could divert the rest of the call to a quick summary of the jobs she and Fran were beginning again, and then turn to Tansy's own concerns: the troubled marriages she was handling as a counsellor, how the children were doing in school and what they did during their spring break at home in Buffalo, still snowy enough for kids' fun.

Setting the receiver back in its cradle, Polly thought over what she had said about the "masterful man." It didn't matter if Tansy had picked up on that or not. She had probably turned him off for good.

"Aren't we lucky to live in the airplane age?" Fran said. "The kids can fly down and see us, and the grandchildren. We can fly up to see them too when they need us."

Polly, still feeling exhausted, said, "It's more likely that we will need them, from now on!"

Both the Andersen boys had come down during spring break, each with a clutch of grandchildren. Both Fran and Polly had a sense of let-down after the exciting visits, so they had walked in the late afternoon through the condominium development to watch the sunset on the shore of Sarasota Bay. Here the mangroves grew thick, their roots anchoring the shoreline. The tops of the mangroves had been trimmed, not enough to break Florida laws, but enough to give a better view of the Bay for people in the nearby dwellings. Roseate spoonbills roosted on the tops of the mangroves, big birds, paler pink than flamingos. How beautiful when they lifted off to fly out over the Bay! The underside of their great stretch of wings showed as a pure strong flamingo pink, the tips of the wings being edged in black, as the whole group whirled in great circles, swooping out over the Bay and away, out toward the Gulf of Mexico. As quickly as some birds flew away from the mangrove roosts, others flew in, to hunch, pale pink, in their sanctuary.

The phone rang later that night: Hal, saying, "Hi, Mom! How would you like it if I flew down next weekend for a very short visit?"

Of course she would love it. "But can you spare the time? Can Mona manage without you?"

"Sure. The big thing is that now I have got my promotion I can set my own time table a little more easily. Friday night at Tampa? Okay?"

Of course okay. But somehow she suspected Tansy's hand behind this sudden and unprecedented visit. Hal and Tansy had no doubt discussed what Loretta's little girl had said at the end of the March break; she could see the script unfolding. Oh, well, a visit from Hal was precious, at any price.

He came out of the elevator at the Tampa airport, stocky and handsome, looking happy and confident. "My rock," as Polly had always thought of him, especially in the days when she had thought of Tansy as "my cross." He tossed his travel bag into the hatchback of Polly's car, wrestling a bit with the recalcitrant handle, duck-taped for security now the lock was gone. "Time you got a new car,

Mom?" But Polly felt the Escort was as dependable now as it had ever been since she bought it eleven years ago, and told him so, firmly. Hal held up his hands. "I'm not about to interfere with you, in anyway," signaling that the old conspiracy to contain Tansy's notions was still in place.

Bill was in his carport, readying a green garbage bag. It was not filled with aluminum dishes any longer, but with the detritus of the grandchildren's visit. He ambled over, hand outstretched. "Hi, Hal! Haven't seen you since your mother moved in – what – four years ago? Five? I hear congratulations are in order. A big promotion?"

"Yes, they've kicked me up onto the management team," Hal laughed. "Director of Development."

"Have you been developing your golf game since you were here last? How about a round tomorrow?" Arrangements were made, for the game, and for dinner afterwards. "Is Capalbo's all right? Do you like pizza?" That set the easy, friendly tone for the weekend.

Two days later, on the way back to Tampa, Hal summarized. "You and Bill are good company for each other."

"Indeed. That's all we are up to – being friends. You can tell Tansy to relax."

"We just don't want you to be hurt, you know."

"Bill and I are not likely to hurt each other, Hal." Hal was ready to take that as proven. Apparently, too, Tansy had not picked up on the mention of the masterful man sufficiently to pass along another alarm to Hal. Polly decided to leave it that way.

-9-   MALLARDS

Time now for the March meeting of the Association. The reconvened general meeting listened quietly to Ginger's revised report. Obviously, Mrs. Morgan and her friends had come prepared to listen in a more open and amiable mood. This time, too, the decorating committee had toned down its proposals. The new palette of rich dark colors would appear, but simply as borders or accents in a generally paler design. The contractors had been placated (no one asked whether that had cost a little or a lot of money). The meeting accepted the report with smug satisfaction, and Ginger was directed to proceed. Polly watched sympathetically as Ginger and her friend Frank DiCaccio shuffled their papers and swatches together in a dispirited way and left the meeting together...

When she went back into her own house, she could see the red light blinking on the answering machine. The message was from Gerald Switzer. He had missed speaking to her at Coffee-Cuppers. He wanted to offer another invitation. This time it was for a seminar on investment, on Thursday at Rosedale. Lunch and a round-table discussion by some well-informed people. He would call back tomorrow to hear if she was free to go with him. This coming Thursday. At noon. "End of message," said the mechanical voice of the answering service.

She would answer yes, Polly decided. She was totally uninformed on investment, but lunch at Rosedale would be nice. An outing with the doctor would keep Mrs. Morgan hot on the gossip trail, but that idea rather appealed to her at this point. So yes. She would say yes.

The lunch was as delicious as expected, and the discussion by well-informed people was as boring as expected. Her host was obviously not bored, however. He concentrated, took notes, and asked an eminently sensible question, to judge by its reception. He was in an affable expansive mood when they began the longish drive home. "I thought you flinched when they discussed the dot-com disasters, Polly. Were you into those high-tech stocks yourself?"

She had to admit she was not into any stocks except for a very small holding in "widow and orphan" companies. She had, she told him, very little to invest in anything, and in any case would never have had the courage to take a flier on anything speculative.

"You're missing a lot of fun," he said seriously, not giving off any hint of knowing what fun was. "Of course conservative investment policy has a lot to be said for it."

"Not by me. I barely meet my obligations. The monthly assessment check just about cleans me out." She spoke lightly so that he could assume that she was joking. He began to comment, but then stopped and changed the subject. That was tactful, she felt; she had no interest in sharing her financial problems with anyone.

He began to tell her about the tennis matches she had missed seeing, then stopped again abruptly, obviously remembering that she had said she had no interest whatsoever in tennis. Better rectify that, she thought. "I do like to watch the final matches at our own Palm Haven courts," she said. "That involves our own friends and acquaintances in a little human drama. Who wins graciously? Who hates to lose? But the fine points escape me."

"Didn't you play when you were young?" He flushed and amended that. "Younger, I mean."

"Nice footwork!" Polly laughed. "Do you think I'm offended by the thought that I'm not young any more, not by a long shot?"

"I think you're very realistic," he said, and added, "It's a thing I admire."

They left both tennis and investment policy behind and drove the rest of the way in what felt like a friendly silence.

Back home, Polly asked whether he would like coffee, or a drink, and they went together out to her lanai. She was a little low on alcohol, but could at least produce peach schnapps and orange juice. He looked rather astonished at the crowded state of her lanai: two patio sets meant eight chairs, plus a Lazy-Boy chair. "That chair makes into a hide-a-bed when my grandchildren come to visit," she explained, and added, "It's crowded I know, but I just keep my eyes on the view." So they settled down into the flowery patio chairs with "fuzzy navels" in hand and looked at the lakeside view.

At this point a little blue-winged teal waddled up from the lake toward the house, then veered and circled back toward the lake. Suddenly it caught sight of another blue-winged dandy who was ushering two small brown females toward the philodendron bushes at the water front. The teal's waddle turned into a hasty rush; undeterred by fierce quacking from the other duck he joined the group and all four hurried into the bushes. "Who will win that round, do you suppose?" Polly asked. But then their attention was deflected to two great gray herons, swooping ferociously after each other with strident calls. Four ibis stalked by, their golden beaks curved toward the ground like tiny scythes. Polly felt that this show was better than tennis, better than talks about investment.

Her companion cleared his throat. "I've been thinking about what you said about your having no investments. I presume you sold all your stocks when you bought this house?"

"Well, no." To her own surprise she found herself explaining, "I didn't buy the house. My son and daughter bought it for me. They're both doing very well now and they insisted I should have a place of my own here where it's warm. I suspect they also figured that was one way to avoid the question of my moving in with one or the other of them."

He looked rather taken aback, then, recovering he said, "It's none of my business, of course. I'm sorry I asked."

"I'm sort of sorry I told you. I don't ever discuss my finances with anyone. I guess it's the drink, and the nice lunch, and the speeches. My defenses are down!"

He didn't seem to know how to handle that one. He turned red with embarrassment, as though one of them had made a faux pas. The blush spread up like a tide, up from the cheeks to the bony forehead and on up the balding dome. He answered hastily, "I'm just sorry the talks weren't as interesting to you as to me. It's been a pleasant afternoon all the same. Thank you for coming."

Her answer was equally trite, "Thank you for inviting me." He departed.

"Mating time for mallards," Fran said next day, and together she and Polly watched as two shiny-headed drakes swam after a dowdy brown duck. A third mallard, iridescent head pitched forward, tried to join the group, but one of the original suitors shot back and drove him away. The brown female had reached the shore and climbed the bank; she now waddled serenely away out of sight, followed at a discreet distance by her two pursuers. "Not so long before she is leading a bevy of little yellow babies down to the water, " Fran said.

"Yes," Polly agreed, but added, "and not so long before the herons sweep down on them and gobble the ducklings up, one at a time."

Fran sighed. "At least you and I aren't worried about any of our ducklings at the moment."

Polly was dubious: Tansy seemed very tense these days, and the old worries were beginning to itch a little. "When do we stop worrying, Fran?"

"When do we stop asking ourselves, 'Where did I go wrong?'" Fran amended, with a sympathetic grin. "Ah, well, not so long before we will all be going north to see how they are really getting along. Checking on the ducklings, and the grand-ducklings."

"At least you are going to your own cottage in July, Fran, where the family can come to visit you. I wish I could do the same. But Tansy and Hal both insist on my staying with them and their families in the summer visits."

"It gets a little claustrophobic, doesn't it?"

Polly laughed. "More than a little!"

"Even in our own cottage we feel a bit hedged in, with all the coming and going, when it suits them, not when it suits us, old stick-in-the-muds that we have become."

"Let's enjoy our independence while we can," Fran said. "Summer is still a couple of months away." The two of them donned dark glasses and sunshade hats and went for a stroll round the lake, following the mallards.

From her lanai, Ginger Elrick called, "Hey you two – mind if I join you?" and the talk turned from matings to meetings. "I think my troubles are over," she said.

At the far end of the lake, a jacaranda spread its mauve lace, and the gnarled branches of the Tree of Gold were now shining with thick clusters of yellow trumpets. Mauve and Gold: Easter colors; soon it would be Easter.

Walking to Coffee-Cuppers next Monday, Polly encountered a swaggering crew of Canada Geese. Memories of an Indiana farm, where geese acted as watch-dogs, frightening a small girl, led her to step cautiously past the domineering flock. Irma caught up with her. "That's one kind of snow-bird everyone in Florida will be glad to see go!"

Polly smiled agreement and the two of them slipped into the clubhouse together.

It turned out to be one of the sad days, when the master of ceremonies had to announce the death of one of the community. Jerome LeBlanc, known to be dying of cancer for several months now, but defeated at last "After a gallant fight."

"They always say that," Irma whispered.

Carl said sadly, "What else is there to say? I don't suppose anyone just gives up and gives in when there's any hope at all of lengthening life."

A quiet discussion ensued, arguments pro and con undergoing distressing chemotherapy, versus accepting the inevitable and rejecting palliation. Who could answer? Who could know what any one individual would choose as the response to this so-frightening eventuality?

These recurring deaths, as in any retirement community, sometimes stirred the survivors to renewed energy in all pursuits.

Certainly there was an unusual energy in Dr. Switzer's voice when he called that noon. An unsettling phone call: Dr. Switzer called to invite her to dinner. "At my place; Amy and John are coming to help me."

Being asked to dinner was not the unsettling bit. No; it was that the idea of helping the doctor raised the specter of that clinic. He explained, however, and the explanation brought a different kind of queasiness. "My sons are coming to visit me over Easter. So I have to get my house in order." Sounds like a funeral call, Polly thought. "Set in order thy house!"

Curiosity outweighed queasiness: no one she knew had ever been invited into Dr. Switzer's house. She looked forward to the evening with some trepidation.

The first surprise came when she was escorted into his house, not through the front door, but around on the lakeside, through the back door into the lanai. "The front door is blocked," he explained.

The Switzer villa was one of the largest in the condominium, and the lanai correspondingly large. It looked huge, however, a big empty space, because all the furniture in it was stored in one corner – as if the owner were about to leave for the summer. "What on earth?"

Before her host could explain the pile-up of chairs and tables, the front door bell sounded, and he dashed back outdoors and around to the front, to bring Amy and John Malone to the lanai entrance. "The front door is blocked," he flung over his shoulder as he sped away.

Amy and John were laughing as they came in. John lifted up one of the lounge chairs and placed it so Amy could sit down. She was still laughing when she said, "Well, we can easily get this room in order, while I explain to poor Polly what this is all about."

While Polly and the two men separated the four stacked chairs and righted the up-ended patio table, Amy spun the tale. "Rusty's sons arranged for a very modish decorator to organize the furnishing and décor of his villa before he moved in. Trouble was, Rusty hated everything the designer did. So as long as his sons don't check up on him, he just pushes all the furniture she chose out of the way, turns the art work to the wall, and gets on with his own kind of life."

They moved into the dining room, ringed again with stacked-up chairs, a table pushed up against the wall, and a sideboard loaded with a pile of paintings. The room was big, made to look even bigger by the fact that the back wall was totally covered by a mirror. "Lift the top picture off the pile, Polly," Amy directed, from her place on one of the handsome dining-room chairs. "It goes on the wall to the left of the mirror."

Polly gasped when she had lifted the painting into place.

"That's the only one Rusty brought with him. All the rest are the decorator's choices," Amy explained. It was a bright, lively scene: a boat on wild water, with a man and two boys and a little girl. All three males were painted as vivid red-heads; the little girl's shiny black hair fanned out behind her with the movement of boat and wind. It was vivid, modern, full of light and life.

"Now I know why –"

"Why he's called Rusty? Yes, that was the way we knew him in the good old days," John smiled. He pulled out another of the dining room chairs for her. "Sit still while I rustle up dinner. We brought a big pot of jambalaya. It just needs a moment in the microwave. We have Portuguese bread and a bottle of burgundy, so we're all set!"

Off he went, leaving Polly and her host to go on with settling the dining-room while Amy directed. "Those two etchings of shore-birds go on the wall facing the mirror, and the sculpture of a heron on the small table under them. The place mats for our supper are in the top drawer of the sideboard, and the big bowls for jambalaya in the side cupboard, the left-hand cupboard."

Supper over, it remained to carry dirty dishes out to the kitchen. It was easy to walk through the living-room, a great empty space, with piled up stuff in the corners; not so easy to get into the kitchen. Here was a forest of potted plants, fig trees, hibiscus, peace lilies, bamboos, philodendron. The doctor's explanation was sheepish. "The decorator believes there should be greenery in every room. But this way it's easy for me to remember to water the damn things."

They pushed through the foliage to the sink, deposited the dishes, and returned to the big job of straightening out the living room. In its center bulked a solitary big black leather chair. It faced an impressive sound system: tape deck, CD player, even an old-style record player. High up at the ceiling in each corner were speakers.

So now the job was to add back all the other furniture. To hang the exciting modern pictures on hangers on each wall, to set out the bits of heavy pottery and sculpture, add the lamps, and to unfurl the small handsome oriental rugs on the shiny tiled floor. Finally the potted trees moved in from the kitchen – the ficus, the philodendron, the bamboo, the hibiscus, each in its own allotted corner.

"A miracle!" Amy cried. "Always a miracle, whenever the boys are due to arrive."

"A miracle because you make it happen, Amy," her friend growled, and then turned to include Polly in his thanks.

"Shall we go on to the bedroom setups?" John asked, and then answered his own question after a glance at Amy, visibly wilting with the excitement and stress of supervising. So the evening ended.

The doctor accompanied Polly the length of the lake and said goodnight at her front door. She slipped back in to her non-decorated, cluttered, dowdy, thoroughly comfortable home.

The next day, Irma phoned. "I wonder if I should invite Bill to my place for Easter dinner, Polly? Or are you planning to spend the day with him yourself?"

Was gossip drifting to Irma from Millie and others, suggesting that Polly's supposed interest in Bill was waning, being replaced by a new direction? Polly could mull over that question later. Meanwhile she must answer the question about Easter. "I have no plans for Easter, Irma."

Irma's follow-up was surprising. "I thought I'd invite him to go to church with me, I notice he drives off to golf on Sunday, same as other days. His own church can't mean much to him. I thought a little real religion might mean a great deal."

The thought of Bill being born again as a Baptist was a bit staggering. Nothing is impossible, Polly thought, so she just said, "If you gave him a home-cooked dinner that would certainly mean a lot to him. We have been finishing up his huge store of frozen TV dinners together, and I bet he'd be thrilled at a change."

"You mean you don't cook for him when he comes over to your place?"

"Certainly not!" Polly laughed. They left it at that.

Carl raised the question of Easter too. "Any plans, Polly? Our young will be with us again, and you know you're always welcome."

Polly hesitated. There had been that odd reference to the two Switzer sons coming for Easter, with the apparent implication that she would be meeting them. But no specific invitation. "I'll have to let you know," she told her friends, unwilling to mention so amorphous an invitation.

No longer amorphous by noon hour. A crisp phone call informed her that all the Switzers would be expecting to take her out for Easter dinner in Sarasota, at the hotel where "the boys" would be staying. "Just the boys" was the added information. "Their families are all apparently too busy with sports teams and school projects and community responsibilities to come to Florida this time."

Her first impulse after hanging up was to call Fran. "What on earth am I to wear? These young men are staying at the Ritz. I haven't a thing that wouldn't embarrass them. And me!"

Fran rose to the occasion. "I'll lend you the outfit I wore for Margie's wedding last summer. You know, sort of silvery gray silk, narrow pants and a long tunic. You could turn over the waist band if you think the pants are too long for you. And you have a long silver chain, haven't you?"

"Oh Fran, that would be so kind of you! You're sure you wouldn't mind lending it to me? I'm just as likely to spill caviar or whatever they serve at the Ritz down the front of your outfit."

"Nonsense," said Fran firmly. "You'll look just right –"

"Sober, pensive and demure?"

"Exactly."

-10-   *HIBISCUS*

Polly caught a glimpse of the younger Switzers on Saturday, striding around the lake with their father. The three were equally tall, and in spite of the difference in ages, equally bald. But the fringe at the back of the two younger heads was unmistakably red. Then they were gone, past her house without a break in the stride, circling to the far end of the lake, and on to the elegantly decorated villa. She wouldn't see them again until tomorrow, Easter Sunday. Sunday at the Ritz.

She was ready for them on Easter, feeling strangely smart in the silvery gray tunic outfit, but also strangely embarrassed – "As if I were misbehaving when I accepted the invitation," she thought. But the young men were deferential, politely handing her into the front seat with their father, and carrying on a light running commentary on the street scenes between Palm Haven and the Sarasota Ritz.

The entertainment did indeed include caviar as an appetizer, in the lounge, with champagne. Polly remained demure during these preliminaries, trying to live up to her (or rather Fran's) sophisticated outfit. But when they moved into the grand dining room they were all more at ease, thanks presumably to the champagne. She noticed, however, that the young Switzers talked a lot, not so much to her as past her, exchanging opinions on Wall Street, politics, medical insurance, and other cheerless topics. Their father made a stiff attempt to include her by swinging the conversation around to tennis, with a dry explanation that Polly didn't like it enough to want to see the Meadowbrook finals. This brought on an astonished silence, quickly ended by a tactful shift back to economic issues. Polly gave up trying to take part in the conversation, and took refuge in a perpetual smile, ladylike, she hoped, but certainly hard on the cheek muscles. · The Ritz was – well – ritzy. The dinner was marvelous: sherried consommé, clever little fillets of perch resting on small hills of julienne vegetables with a sprig of rosemary gallantly furled as decoration. Chocolate mousse, again a small serving, drizzled with raspberry coulis, and daintily surrounded with tiny dots of chocolate and whipped cream. All the right wines. And all the wrong conversation. The three men argued in very quiet, very scathing tones about virtually every topic, interspersed with intermittent polite and futile efforts to make their guest feel at ease. Ease was certainly not the keynote.

Coming back to the Switzer villa after dinner for a cup of coffee (and a small glass of port for the men), they found the house in full glory, with Easter flowers and decorations on the coffee table and side tables. Some of the decorations were garish, folk art sharply out of key with the subdued richness of the other appointments in the room. "We dug out Father's Portuguese chanticleers, stuff he used to have in his villa in Portugal," said David, the younger of the sons, (sounding much more human than he had at any point in the Ritz dinner). "Not that any of it goes with what the decorator had in mind."

"I didn't know you spent time in Portugal," Polly said with a faint rush of nostalgia for her own little Portuguese tour. David smiled, a little grimly. "Our mother didn't like Portugal, but Father was a real sucker for the language, the food, and the general atmosphere."

"Oh, I loved Portugal!" Polly cried. "My son Hal promises to take me there again, some day." Then, as if the combination of tension, good wines, and a yearning for another time with her own son urged her into abnormal talkativeness, she went on, "Portuguese is one of Hal's best languages, and he'd like a chance to practice in a casual setting. Hal did linguistics in University, you know," (but of course they couldn't know, a little voice in the back of her head warned). "Then he switched into computer science. So he's a computer linguist, apparently a very good thing to be, especially in Raleigh. Near Raleigh is a sort of Silicon Valley of the east coast, you know. Clever young people from all over the world are drawn there, and although they are experts in programming, they don't speak ordinary English. So Hal runs ESL classes in his spare time, though he hasn't much of that. He's very very busy, to the point of feeling burnt out."

All three of the Switzer men looked rather astonished at this eruption into speech. Finally Graham, the lawyer son, said stiffly, "How very interesting."

Miffed by his tone, Polly promptly stood up, thanked all three for a delicious dinner, and prepared to go home.

The doctor, silent as he drove her back to her villa, broke out as they pulled into her drive way, "My sons are not noted for their interpersonal skills."

(Rather what people said about him, Polly thought,)

He slipped into an apologetic tone. "Could I ask you to help us put things back once the boys have gone?"

"You mean to strip down to the essentials again?"

"Yes. I can't manage with just John; Amy is simply not able to lend a hand at all."

"She's very gallant," Polly offered.

She was rewarded with a very warm smile. "Salt of the earth. Always has been. Anyway, goodnight for now. I'll phone you on Tuesday and see if you can spare time for the reverse furniture moving."

Polly woke up next morning to the clatter of machines. The condominium team was here already, intent on doing the late spring chores. Two men were edging her garden, two others were spreading a heavy load of mulch, some of it downing her smaller flowers, the alyssum and impatiens. Another worker was power-clipping the hibiscus, the copper bush, and the flame-of-the-forest. When she was here in her first Florida spring, Polly had dashed out and tried to deter them. "That hibiscus is loaded with buds!" she had cried. "You're destroying it!" They had smiled and continued the work, and when she phoned the office she was given assurances that this was the right way for Florida; that next year the hibiscus would be stronger than ever. "More buds! More flowers!" In her second spring she had recognized the results of the system. Indeed, here was yet another example of how different this environment was from her home region. "I'm too old for all these different systems," she had thought, until her spirits flared up in denial. "Never too old! Or at least not yet!" This morning, hearing the shears and the edgers, she turned over and slipped into a last dreamy slumber before it was time to join her new world at the clubhouse.

On the way to Coffee-Cuppers, Polly pushed her way through a phalanx of Canada geese parading along the lakeside walk. More of them were gathering every day, making connections for the long trip north, and meanwhile making life in the south unpleasant for those not yet ready to wing it away. Most of the human walkers stepped aside, implicitly ceding ground to a more domineering species.

On the lake itself there were now many birds: cootes, scaup, gulls, anhinga. Gawky pelicans still plunged to an awkward landing, settling as if unaware into the center of flocks of smaller birds and dispersing them. Far overhead, three big black frigate birds soared, their tails flaring out, swallow-fashion, into scissor points, their shadows somehow menacing on the lake's surface. At the water's edge, waders moved: egrets, along with white, little blue and great blue herons. The bird life was infinitely interesting, and still novel to a former inland northern dweller.

Dawdling to watch them, Polly decided there was no point hurrying to the club house: Carl had phoned early in the morning to say he and Fran would not be going to the weekly gathering. "We're both still tired after the onslaught of grandchildren during March break. Fran is really exhausted. I think she needs a day in bed, in fact."

Not like Fran.

Irma was missing from Coffee-Cuppers too. She had decided to undergo another little cosmetic operation – a neck lift, and was hunkering out of sight for the time being.

Third, Jackson Elrick was absent. Ginger said casually that he had decided to spend Easter with his grandchildren, and would not be back for a while.

Fourth, there was no sign of Gerald Switzer. Probably his sons were still here, or else needing a lift to Tampa to the airport.

John Malone came across to the table and sat in one of the empty chairs. "Rusty asked me to tell you we won't need to work at reinstating his furniture. He's decided to hire a moving company. Good idea, of course; we're all getting a little long in the tooth for that kind of job. Besides, we are becoming very busy at the clinic, and neither of us has any energy to spare."

Polly asked with minimum politeness about the clinic.

"We have a whooping-cough epidemic on our hands," John Malone replied. "Keeping us both busy, full time. We're trying a little experiment with a new regimen. In fact," he hitched his chair closer, "confidentially, we plan to write a paper about our experiment. Our final co-authored paper, probably, last of a long series." Polly murmured congratulations, and unleashed a further bit of information.

"We'll need someone to type and edit it. Can you type?"

"Yes I can type," said Polly. "But I don't want to get involved." (Rather graceless, she thought later, and rather silly. It might have been fun to play a part in an experiment aimed at improving the health of little children, and not as a nurse. Dr. Malone didn't seem affronted. "I have another favor to ask you," he said, "a personal one. It's Amy. While I am so busy at the clinic every day right now, she's on her own. The worst thing is that she's run out of reading material."

"Do you want me to get her some books from the library?"

"Better still, could you take her there? It's just a matter of helping her in and out of the car, you know."

Polly did know: her own mother had been crippled with arthritis. "I'll be glad to," she said, and thought, "That should ease my conscience about not helping at the clinic – not that my conscience is all that active these days!"

John Malone said a grateful goodbye, leaving her free to go.

She was eager to talk this request over with Fran. She must also tell Fran that the Easter gray silk outfit had been successful, and was still unmarred by caviar.

She walked toward Fran's house.

The blinds in the lakeside bedroom were drawn and there was no sign of either of her friends on their lanai. She continued homeward, more slowly.

Canada geese still lurked in front of her own house, treading through her new Easter lilies. While she was shooing them (gingerly) away, Bill called across to ask whether she would like him to come over for their habitual supper. She was curious to hear how he had got along with Irma, and amused when he offered, "I have some nice leftovers from Easter dinner, ham and all that. We should have something better than the frozen TV dinners this evening."

Sure enough, the leftovers were delicious.

"So long since I had a home-cooked meal!"

Polly pretended indignation. "C'mon, Bill, I cook for you occasionally!"

"Of course. You made pancakes on Shrove Tuesday –"

And yes, that was indeed the extent of the home cooking she had been offering her nice neighbor.

In the second week after Easter, Bill had company again. Loretta had descended, slipping down to Florida for a weekend for a quick check up on her father. Coming to Polly's place, within minutes of arrival, smiling ingratiatingly, she asked, "What's going on with Daddy and this Irma person?"

Polly could only shrug and plead ignorance.

"He seems to be seeing her very often. Very very often."

"I hope so," Polly found herself saying. "He needs all the company he can get. He's a very sociable man." Then, "Have you met Irma?"

"No. Well, just at mother's funeral I guess, but we don't remember her. Now it seems she's temporarily disappeared."

Polly decided not to explain about the post-Easter neck-lift. "Irma's a really sweet woman," she said.

"We thought you and Daddy –" No end to that sentence.

Better put an end to the implication; Polly said firmly, "No. We have nice suppers together and watch TV. We both think it's better than being alone. We like each other. That's it, Loretta. That's it."

"Surely you could prevent him from seeing so much of Irma, even if only as a friend?"

"Why?"

"Well – she's taking him to church and to prayer meetings."

"So?"

Loretta looked surprised at Polly's impercipience. "We're Catholics, as you very well know."

Polly couldn't resist. "Irma would say Bill is a Christian, and so is she."

"Oh, yes, of course." A small doubt crept into the young voice. "I guess we just want him to be happy. It's just that we thought that he's safer with you."

Polly laughed and said, "I'm not a Catholic, Loretta."

Loretta was unfazed. "You're Episcopalian, though, and that seems harmless. Not a Baptist at any rate."

"I'm not much of anything anymore, Loretta. Surely anything is better than nothing, when it comes to faith."

Loretta didn't look at all ready to accept this proposition. Her voice was still uncertain when she reiterated, "We just want him to be happy."

Polly stretched out a hand. "You're a good daughter, Loretta. In the end we just have to let things take care of themselves."

Loretta stood up. "I don't accept that, Polly, any more than I would let my children's lives take care of themselves."

Polly gave a small sigh. "It isn't always a matter of 'letting'."

After a restless night, Polly woke before dawn, and was rewarded with the experience of a glorious Florida sunrise. The whole sky glowed, amber and coral. Black against this splendor, the tall Norfolk Island Pine stood across the road. In its topmost branches was an osprey nest. Already the big birds soared and swooped, foraging for food for the nestlings. Polly could see the agitation of tiny bodies in the cusp of the pine. She sighed, remembering her own long-ago early mornings and the rush to satisfy the cries of her young. The birds would never know the reverse of this period, she thought, sadly. Among humans, on the other hand, there came a time when the young fostered the old. They fostered and worried and bullied the parents; there was no instinct for that phase among the strong young birds that would soon be flying from the nest.

Now at least she had an easier life, flocking with friends her own age, troubled only occasionally by pangs of regret for opportunities missed when the children were young, and consoled, more often, by the comfort of knowing that they did worry about her, bless their hearts. Ah well, time to go back indoors, to get ready for the weekly flocking together of the silver-feathered birds of Palm Haven.

Although Irma was back at Coffee-Cuppers, sporting a pink turtle-necked T-shirt, Fran again didn't turn up. Still not feeling very well, Carl explained, and he thought she should call off the Meals-on-Wheels work for the time being. Maybe someone else would fill in? It turned out that both the Vanderburgs, the other youngish newcomers who sometimes sat at their table, had been wondering what they could get into, as a volunteer effort for the community. They offered to help Polly this week. "Fran should back off for a while," Carl advised. "Why don't the three of you just carry on for now?" To Polly, as they left the hall, he said, "Drop in for a minute as usual, Polly. But don't stay too long. She's really rather miserable."

To Polly, Frances looked miserable indeed. Not pale – no one could look pale in Florida – the tan was too firmly in place for that. Fran was always thin, but she was clearly too thin now. She did look sick. Fran was determined that no one should worry. "I just had a sudden pain this morning." Polly was afraid to ask if Fran suspected a recurrence of cancer. She had been in remission for three years, after a scare ended with successful (and sickening) chemotherapy.

Carl was giving nothing away as he chatted determinedly about the news Fran had missed at Coffee-Cuppers. He asked Polly with a smile, "What about your latest date with the doctor?"

Yes, she had gone to another Van Wezel concert with him but she found it hard to tell Carl and Frances about the experience. "Mozart this time," he had said, "I won't be as wildly responsive as that other time." He had sounded sheepish, and she had realized it took grim self-discipline for him to mention that earlier display of what he would call weakness, though she had dubbed it "being human." This time there had been no emotional repercussion during the concert. Nevertheless on the way home he had abruptly recalled that earlier moment. "I lied to you last time we went to the symphony," he had said. "About my reaction to the Mahler, the song in the last movement. It isn't just the general pathos of that song that distresses me. It makes me think of my own daughter. No – she didn't die, like the singer of the song; but she might as well be dead, for all the connection with me she allows. She has married twice, and each time she has expected me to give her away. That's the extent of her interest in me, her affection or concern. I think that's why that song sweeps over me with such sadness. Such a sense of loss. Not death but a kind of death in life." His hands had been tight and white on the steering wheel. "I don't know why I'm telling you this. I guess I thought you might always wonder about my breakdown that other time."

Polly could think of no appropriate way to acknowledge his revelation. Of course she couldn't tell Fran and Carl all this – too private, too difficult to explain.

Carl, unaware of her disturbance, was in a teasing mood about the outing. He kept the conversation going; Fran made no response.

Polly stayed a moment longer, then she left. There was a niggling little fear in her heart about Fran's state of health.

-11-   ON THE BEACH

Whatever Polly's dark mood, it was a lovely sunny April day. The color of the Tree of Gold was reflected in the smooth surface of the lake. Polly's garden flourished with the same bright color, golden marigolds, backed by the yellow hibiscus bushes, in full bloom again. Still, there were shadows in her mind: a little embarrassment lingering from the slightly awkward evening of Mozart; a little unease about Loretta's visit, somewhat bothersome; a half-irritation as she waited for Tansy's weekly phone call with its inevitable questioning and advice ("though of course it's just her concern about me"); and beneath those thoughts the echo of Carl's words about Fran: "She's really rather miserable."

Late that same night, Carl was on the phone, in a panic. "Something is terribly wrong with Fran. Can you come over? She should be in the hospital, but she's fighting to stop me from taking her there. I can't control her alone. Could you come? Maybe even ask Bill, so that if one of us is driving the other could hold Fran still."

Bill was out. Polly could see that there was no car in his driveway. Without conscious decision she found herself dialing the Switzer number, pouring out the trouble to an apparently half-awake doctor, and feeling vastly reassured when he said. "I'll be over to the Andersens' house as fast as I can make it."

He arrived there almost as quickly as Polly. Fran was doubled up, in obvious pain, but fighting fiercely against Carl's efforts to calm her. Dr. Switzer opened his bag. "I'm going to give her something to relieve the pain and calm her down. She's hysterical, and exhausting herself."

Carl cried, "She seems to be in terrible pain. You know she's in remission from cancer –"

The doctor cut in. "This has nothing to do with cancer. This kind of sudden attack is gall bladder probably, or maybe kidney; I can only take a guess. We must get her to the hospital right away. Should I call an ambulance?"

Even while Carl was answering that it would be quicker to take their own car, the doctor was steadying Fran, holding her hands, all the while talking to her quietly, gently, so that her resistance diminished and she said in a very small voice, "I've thought all day that it was the cancer coming back. And then tonight –"

"No, no, my dear. This kind of sudden trauma, not at all likely," and the two watchers could see the visible release of tension.

"I couldn't help her," Carl said, visibly distressed.

"Easier for me," the doctor answered. "Special mark of a pediatrician, calming frightened patients." He was helping Fran stand, supported by Polly, while Carl put a jacket around her shoulders. "I'm good at slipping a needle into very small veins too," he added, apparently in all seriousness.

Together they helped Fran into the car, putting her in the back seat so Polly could steady her. The doctor would follow in his own car. For Polly the whole business of getting Fran to the hospital carried ominous, ominous echoes of the night eight months ago when they had maneuvered Elnora into an ambulance and followed to the hospital. That time it was just a case of a sick, unfriendly neighbor. Now it was Fran, dearest Fran. Please let it be something relatively simple like a gall bladder attack! Polly knew that if it was gall-stones, Fran would have to endure the excruciating pain until the attack had spent its own fury, since no one would want to operate while the attack was in progress, but let it be that, painful as it might be, and not a perforated ulcer, not a heart attack. She was confident enough in the doctor's diagnosis not to be afraid of cancer now.

In the emergency room and in the little cubicle where the nursing aide settled Fran for the moment, Dr. Switzer's authority made itself felt. He stayed with the Resident who came in to do an examination, shooing Carl and Polly back into the waiting room.

When he came out to tell them what was going on, he looked happier and less worried. "Gall bladder, right enough. Severe enough that they want to operate as soon as it's safe. Probably tomorrow they will start prepping her. Meanwhile she's being admitted. Carl will want to stay on, but you and I," he reached a hand to pull Polly to her feet, "should go home and get some sleep."

They were both yawning when he turned his car into her driveway. "There's nothing we can do for Frances right now," he said. "Maybe we could do something together tomorrow, so you could keep your mind off her troubles. I'll call you."

It was eleven o'clock before she woke up, or rather was wakened by the phone ringing. "Gerald speaking."

Gerald? Of course, but she had never called him anything except Dr. Switzer or "you". Whatever his name, he sounded bright and eager. "Let's take a picnic and go to the beach. Right now."

"Well yes, that might be a good idea." But Polly couldn't let the business of a name just slide by. She had to go on, "I know your friends call you Rusty. But I never thought it was appropriate."

He laughed ruefully. "No, I'm not a red-head any more. Nothing rusty left. In fact not much of anything left."

She pictured the high dome fringed with gray hair, carefully barbered, righteously combed, but still, rather thin, and certainly not rusty, and silently agreed. ("But he doesn't look so bony anymore," she thought. Maybe he was eating better now. Something was making him look less cadaverous.

Meanwhile he was saying, slowly, "My mother called me Jeronimo. I was a great jumper, and fighter. I was a naughty child, I guess."

That was hard to believe. Still, maybe Jeronimo would be easier to say than Gerald, or Rusty. However, "Most nicknames are shorter than the real names. Jeronimo is – "

"An elongation? I guess so."

It was hard to think of him as a little boy, with a mother who whimsically elongated his name. She found herself asking, "Were you an only child?"

"Yes. And you?"

Polly told him about her sister Carol in California.

He had had enough of this conversation. "What about the idea of a picnic, Polly? It will be a break from worrying about Fran. Okay?"

"Okay," Polly said, but found she couldn't quite add "Gerald". "Okay. A picnic would be just fine."

By noon they were going along Cortez Avenue, lined with frothing bougainvillea, toward the bridge to Anna Maria Island. Turning left to Coquina Beach, they parked in the long row of cars and vans and trucks, carried the small cooler to the nearest table, and settled in for a quiet time.

"I brought the paper," he said.

"So did I".

It turned out they took papers of the opposite political stripe. He read with an occasional "humph" and "ha-ha", but it didn't seem wise to ask why; no point in stirring up muddy waters. She suppressed her own "humphs", and turned to the comics. "Do you like `For Better or for Worse?'"

"I prefer `Dilbert'."

The quiet settled down, and the heat. Silence. Perfect silence. Even the cicadas had ceased their high whine. The trees stood still, the Australia pines, the palm trees. Not a breath stirring.

Then softly, a breeze came from nowhere, stirring the fronds. The cicadas began again their high shrill song.

The sun soaked in. The breeze cooled off. The papers dropped to the sandy ground. There was calm in nature, and calm of mind. Groggy with the heat and the anticlimax after last night's tension, Polly remembered that phrase from long-ago memory work: "calm of mind, all passion spent." Funny thing to have made teenagers memorize, she thought. Lovely line, for now, for this moment, this peaceful interlude; peace, perfect peace.

She was asleep.

After – how long? maybe only ten minutes or so, but maybe half an hour, she slipped quietly back into consciousness, found herself watching her companion as he stood by the shore, watching the birds. He seemed to sense that she was awake again, and strode back toward her, with determination in his aspect.

"I want to ask you something. Take your time about answering."

A little chilly breeze seemed to flutter the pine trees above their table. Polly sat up, not really ready for serious discussion.

The question, when it came, was sharp. "Would you come back to the clinic with me?"

The answer was easy. "No."

"I don't understand you.," he said. "You're a good nurse."

Polly sat up straight, ready to fight. "I'm not. I went into nursing only because my parents thought it would be a nice job for a girl. I married Harold just before I graduated, secretly, of course, and I thought with relief that I'd never work in the wards again." (Why am I telling him all this? she wondered, but having begun, she seemed impelled to go on.) "I found I was pregnant before I could get a job doing anything else. Then Harold was away so much I took on the easiest thing I could find: private nursing, night duty. I couldn't really enjoy Tansy when she was a baby, because I was always sleepy and tired. Just when Harold left for good, I found I was pregnant again. Then I really did have to go at the nursing as a business. I could have gone back to my family in Indiana I guess, but they didn't really relish the idea, I could tell from their voices." Polly laughed. It was all so long ago, not forgotten, but not a matter of bitterness now that all the struggle was over. "We soldiered on, the kids and I, supported by whatever nursing job turned up. The happiest was in obstetrics, so I stuck to that longest, but I never enjoyed it. At last the kids were settled and successful, and I could retire." She stopped, amazed at the long tumble of memories, all condensed into so few sentences. She concluded, wryly, "This is a long version of 'no', in answer to your question!"

Instead of arguing, he began to pack up the cooler, folded his chair and his paper, and watched in silence while she followed suit.

That afternoon, one of the multitude of phone calls inquiring about Fran's progress came from Millie Morgan. Having shown her concern, however, this caller switched rather gleefully to her own choice of topic. "I presume you've heard the news about your other friend, Ginger Elrick?"

The switch was too swift for sad and tired Polly. "What?"

"It seems that her husband has left her. I have a friend in Venice, who heard from Mrs. Elrick's friend there. Mr. Elrick has told his daughter and son-in-law that he is not coming back here. Sick and tired of the place." An audible sniff. "I must say he didn't give Palm Haven much of a chance. They have only been here – what – two years?"

"That's right."

"Who can blame him? She has been so obsessed with all this committee business. That other man, De Coochy, I hear he's at her place at all hours of the day and night. I must say –"

But Polly felt that she must say something instead. She was too weary to cope with this gossip. "I'm so sorry, Millie, but I must hang up. I'm waiting to call Carl now, to compare notes with him about Fran."

"Oh, well, of course you must. But –"

But Polly had hung up. Fran's needs were too pressing to permit any side-tracks.

Hal phoned on Thursday. Astonishing! He was again coming down to see her. "Tansy thought that one of us should be with you for a bit, while you're so worried about Aunt Fran."

"So you're the `one of us'," Polly laughed. Privately she thought that although Tansy's phone call this week had shown shock and worry about Fran's illness, the call had held an undertone of worry of a different kind. All those details about calling the doctor in the middle of the night and going picnicking with him the next day: Tansy's antenna had picked up something new. She had winkled out the count of outings, symphonies, seminars, dinner at the Ritz. Hal, the "one of us" coming to support Mom, was also deputed to see how the land lay, insofar as Gerald was concerned. (Polly had to admit to herself that she had no idea how the land lay, but was as delighted as ever to have a second unexpected visit from darling Hal.)

Next evening, driving Hal home from the airport over the Sunshine Bridge, she took the bull by the horns. "I think we should invite Dr. Switzer out to dinner. He's been so marvelous about

Fran, and I owe him a return for the Easter dinner he treated me to, when his sons were here."

The doctor had forestalled her. There was a clipped message on the answering machine. "I hope you and your son will have dinner with me tomorrow. I've reserved at the Café des Arts for 6:30. Please let me know if that is not agreeable to you."

Hal made no comment. "Now tell me about Auntie Fran," he said.

Before she could answer, the phone rang. Bill was calling from next door to speak to Hal. "Welcome again, Hal! Any chance of a game of golf tomorrow?"

A regretful no. "Going to spend as much time as I can at the hospital with Frances Andersen."

"Of course."

"How about Sunday morning, though?" Hal countered.

Rather sheepish, Bill explained he was going to church with Irma, and then on to dinner with her at her house. "Sorry."

Catholic Bill, set for a Baptist Sunday! Something for Hal to tell Tansy, Polly thought. Maybe that would calm down her concerns about Bill Magee, though maybe, on the other hand, that would sharpen her focus on Gerald Switzer. It was unfair to Tansy to think this way, Polly knew. Tansy was tense and excitable, but so bonded to her mother and brother she could hardly concentrate on her own children. "We were together too much for too long, against the world most of the time. No wonder Tansy is anxious," Polly thought, "and loving. And protective." Then an unexpected little afterthought. "I wish she could meet Gerald. Wonder how they would get along?" She found no obvious answer.

Instead, she phoned Carl, to get the latest news on Frances and to plan for Hal's time with her tomorrow.

Having Hal available to drive Polly back and forth to the hospital and to share the visits to Fran gave Carl a little breathing space. For Polly and Hal, at the end of a long day at the hospital, brief visits interspersed with long spells of sitting in the waiting room so that Fran could sleep and rest, the thought of a good dinner at the Café des Arts was very welcome.

As he swung the car into the parking lot, the doctor explained to Hal, "Since you're a linguist, I thought you'd like this restaurant. You can practice your French on the chef."

Hal laughed; Polly, belatedly, joined in. A joke. Not Gerald's norm; she wasn't ready for it.

The talk did indeed turn to linguistics as course after delectable course appeared. Gerald announced, "One of my great interests when I was a practicing pediatrician was the development of language in early childhood. The anatomy of speech, the development of tongue and palate, jaws, all the physical apparatus that the mind must learn to control, as the ability to speak develops: that fascinated me."

Fascinating, Hal agreed, and he had indeed been reading something along that line lately, "By a Dr. Feldstein, I think?"

Indeed it was, and the two men enjoyed a rapid fire exchange of questions and answers, to find out where their expertise overlapped. The mood was as jovial as when the Malones had stage-managed the set-up of Gerald's furniture, just before Easter.

Then the formal curtain descended again. The doctor said quietly, as they drove home, "I know you don't want to work at the clinic again. But can I assume that you are considering our need of your help on the whooping-cough report?"

Polly thought rebelliously that he must realize she had said no when John Malone asked for that help; but now she heard herself saying meekly, "Yes. Yes, I am considering it."

Hal had observed her flustered response. "He seems to be a bit of a control-freak," he said after they had been deposited at home. "Deciding that we would go out with him and choosing the restaurant. Announcing to you what you are to consider." Then he laughed. "Nice man, though. Very interesting."

The weekend flew by, and Hal departed, chauffeured to Tampa early Monday morning by Gerald, who had phoned with orders: "I will drive your son to the airport. That way you will be less tired tomorrow to help Fran get ready to go home from the hospital."

As the two men pulled out of the driveway, Polly realized how tired she was, from the double strain of entertaining Hal and visiting Fran. But it was time for the inevitable Coffee-Cuppers, and she felt she mustn't break her ordinary routine. Remembering her conversation with John Malone – what? Two weeks ago? – she also realized with a little pang of guilt that she had promised to help Amy Malone, and had not done so. She would talk to John this morning, or phone, and make a date with Amy for Wednesday.

After a quiet coffee hour, Polly left the clubhouse, drifted along the alligator-free lakeshore, and stopped in at Fran and Carl's place. Carl was busy rearranging the villa so as to make things more comfortable for Fran, moving a couch out to the lanai so that she could watch the birds while convalescing, reorganizing the kitchen "for my own convenience as temporary chief cook and bottle washer," he laughed. "Please stay for lunch, Polly and test my salmon quiche. I'm practising now, so I can do it right this evening after we bring Fran home."

But Polly had to get back to her own house in time for Tansy's weekly call. This time she forestalled questions about the masterful man by quickly telling Tansy about her promise to take Amy Malone to the library to pick up some books, and consulting Tansy about what books her Buffalo book group had chosen for study this spring. The phone call ended in unusual accord. "Give my dearest love to Aunt Fran."

-12-   *AMARYLLIS*

Amaryllis and Africa lilies were blooming in Amy Malone's garden when Polly came to pick her up. With a walker, Amy managed to move to Polly's car, but getting into the car was something else, a difficulty to be repeated when they reached the library. "Actually, you are dealing with me better than John does," Amy gasped, when they were finally moving through the automatic doors. "That's your nursing training, I bet!"

"You should know," Polly grinned, for they had shared a few more comic profesional memories as they drove along Manatee Avenue.

The pleasantest part of the outing was the discovery that they shared their taste in books. They both took out books by women named Ann: Ann Tyler, Ann Patchett, Anne Perry. "And Annie Proulx," Amy added. They also confessed that "Anne of Green

Gables" had been a favorite when they were young girls, one in Indiana, the other in Connecticut. Both were beaming in happy memories of the joys of reading when they arrived back in Palm Haven.

Amy put her hand on the door handle, and then paused before opening the door. "I can't let you go without saying thank you, Polly – for the change you're making in Rusty. He's happier than he has been for thirty – no, forty years. I guess you've figured out that his marriage was not a happy one?"

Polly smiled, in a noncommittal way. But Amy was not about to follow that tack. Instead she said, "I want to tell you what he has done for us. He pulled John and me out of a worse mess than anything he himself ever faced. We had a child – our son got into dreadful trouble, drugs and all that, you know – and Rusty helped us through everything, right up to the end. It's complicated: our son was adopted, and it was Rusty that found him for us when we found I couldn't have children, so he pretended he felt responsible for young Gerald. But he went way beyond any responsibility; way beyond. . . " Amy broke off for a second, then resumed with a shaky smile, "I didn't want to get into all this. Just to say how much it means to us to see Rusty laughing with you, phoning you, coming out of his shell."

"You're very good friends, the three of you," Polly said, "Like Fran and Carl and me. I do know what it's like to have been helped, way beyond what anyone could expect." She couldn't quite begin to tell Amy what the Andersens had done for her during the bad years with Harold. Time enough later; she realized what it had cost Amy to tell part of her story, and knew it would not make the effort easier if she tried to match it with her own. So she just said,"We've both been lucky, you and I."

s she watched her new friend struggle back up the path, Polly thought, "I'm learning a new alphabet in Florida, starting with "A": Amy, amaryllis, anhingas. Alligators too, of course." Strange, how quickly one responded to new things here. Like the sudden spurts of growth in this fostering sunshine, human emotions seemed speeded up. Friendship, for instance: this time last year she had hardly known Amy and Irma, Ginger, and Millie Morgan. Now she felt deeply concerned in their lives. They, too, were experiencing sudden new emotions. For instance, Irma and Bill, mere acquaintances so recently, were now tangled into a knot of changing religions. Her mind shied away from that other sudden growth, her relationship with angular Gerald Switzer, much harder to categorize than the predictable attraction between amiable Bill and pretty, protectable Irma.

Then her thoughts swung to the opposite extreme: old friendships. She remembered her mother's old song, learned long ago at Women's Institute meetings: "Make new friends, but keep the old!/ One is silver, and the other, gold." Watching silvery Amy moving on her chrome walker, Polly thought of Fran, almost back in golden good health, and still the dearest of all.

She had hardly parked her car in the carport when she heard the phone ring and hurried in. Gerald was calling to arrange another trip to the beach. "I have something to tell you."

The something concerned his family. He parked the car carefully, led the way to the edge of the surf, began to pace along, just above the water's edge. "It's my daughter. I had a phone call last night." His voice sounded portentous, and also amazed.

"Wonderful! You said you never hear from her. This is wonderful – isn't it?" Polly remembered the vivid painting she had seen in his living room: the man and his three children in a sailboat, two red-headed boys and the one little girl, her shiny black hair blowing in the wind.

"I guess it's a good thing. She sounded very stiff; cross and not friendly at all." He stopped and turned to her. He was blushing – a slow flush that crept upward from chin to cheekbone. He clutched his forehead as if to stop the embarrassing tide. "She had heard from the boys, I guess, about – about you – that you and I were seeing a lot of each other. They quizzed me when they were here, you know. I suppose I was not as discreet as I should have been. Anyway, they told Lynne about you."

"There's nothing to tell!" But Polly knew there was plenty to tell, remembering how Tansy's tally of their outings together had brought Hal down to check on her. "Anyway, Lynne is coming to Florida for a weekend. This weekend."

Polly remembered the hurried prelude to "the boys' " visit. "Will you go through all that performance of changing your house again?"

He shucked off the suggestion. His daughter had had nothing to do with the decorator's doings, and she would not care whether his place was smart or dowdy, ugly or stylish.

Polly walked across the sand with him in silence, remembering again the beautiful little girl in the picture. Again, as so often, it seemed, he guessed at what she was thinking. "Lynne looks like her mother. The eyes. The beautiful black hair."

An old song came into Polly's mind. "Black – black – black is the color of my true love's hair – " Could anyone, she wondered, ever replace that first true love, even when that first love had turned out to be untrustworthy, like Harold? Or hard and contemptuous, as Gerald's wife presumably had been? Suddenly she asked, "Is your wife alive?"

He was startled. "Of course. Married again, not very happily, I gather. Lynne turned against me long before that. It was my fault. I seemed indifferent to her."

"You weren't. You still are not."

"No."

Polly found herself silenced. Her thoughts swung wildly to find a way that she could help him move away from the lonely and hurtful memories. There was one small way of pleasing him, at least. She heard herself saying, "I would like to help you with your report, after all. If I can."

Without wondering what had brought about this change in her, he fell at once into masterful mode. "Excellent!" He swung at once into an explanationn about what he and John were studying and concluded, "The epidemic is dying, so we are ready to complete our article. We have big stacks of data already. I have the papers piled up in my lanai but we aren't sure how to sort it."

"I could do that," Polly offered. "It's kind of what I did when I was called a file clerk in my last year at the hospital. Actually I was classifying research material, sifting it into categories."

"Perfect. Of course you would need desk space, maybe a computer. I could fit out my dining-room as a sort of office for you."

And what would the hostile daughter think, Polly wondered, if she came to Florida and found me installed in her father's dining-room, working on his project?

We'll just have to wait and see, she decided. Meanwhile, the beach stretched before them and they resumed their walk. "Why don't you take off your shoes?" she asked. She had long ago rolled up her pant legs and dropped her sneakers into the blue beach bag.

He looked startled for a minute. Then he said, "I loved going barefoot on the beach in Cape Cod when I was little," and took off his shoes.

"Lucky you!" Polly laughed. "In Indiana all we could do was dream about the ocean!"

The Gulf of Mexico rolled its waters beside them in every shade of blue and green, with a line of purple at the horizon. The sand beach swept beyond and behind them in a great white curve, and the wet sand squished between their toes.

"A very good idea, going barefoot," he opined. "Sand is excellent for massaging the arches. A good light abrasive for the skin too." How to respond to that? They finished their beach walk in silence.

When Polly came back from Fran's house two days later, a snow-white egret was standing tall on the patio apron. Lacy white tail feathers ruffed in the little wind, and the long head feathers floated up and back, just like a bride's veil. The elegant bird looked Polly over and then daintily made its unhurried way back to the lake shore.

Bill's car was driving into his place, followed by a little yellow Volkswagen Beetle. Out of it stepped a big black figure. Bill got out of his car, turned, shook hands with the other man, and gestured him toward the house. Polly recognized the priest who had officiated at Elnora's funeral. A pastoral call, then, formal enough that the priest was wearing his clerical collar.

Polly went back to her kitchen and put on a wash. She noticed that the little yellow car was still at Bill's place when it was time to change the wash into the dryer. Finally, when she was folding the dried shirts and tea towels and pillow slip, Bill and his guest came out into the drive, shook hands, and then the big priest collapsed himself into the little car and drove away.

Bill wandered over a little early for the dinner they had arranged to share. After an exchange of question and answer about Fran's progress, he said, "Father Ben from Sts. Peter and Paul came to see me today."

Polly admitted to watching the priest come and go. She waited for further comment.

Bill said, "He says he's been missing me at church. Seems he's not happy about me going to the Baptist services. He was very affable, but I felt he was really disturbed and sorry."

"What will you do about it, Bill?"

He hesitated. "I guess I'll quit going to the Baptist service. I didn't like it very much, anyway. But Irma's such a sweet little person, I hate to disappoint her."

"Wouldn't she go to your church with you, Bill?"

"Don't think so." Then he repeated, "She's such a pretty little thing."

(So the big blue eyes and the newly swan-like neck were having their desired effect, Polly thought.) She changed the subject. "Would you like a beer? Or a rum and coke?"

"I'm a little bothered by all this," he answered. "I guess it calls for rum."

So rum it was, followed by a rather dry TV dinner of Swiss steak and noodles.

The next day, Irma weighed in on the subject while she and Polly were doing a tour of the lake. "I'm going to go with Bill this afternoon to the Saturday service at his church. He says it's quite informal. No incense. I hate incense."

It sounded like the thin edge of the wedge to Polly, but she said neutrally, "No harm in going to the service and seeing how you like it." Then she changed the subject, asking whether Irma had seen anything of Ginger, who seemed to be invisible lately.

Irma said no, but added slowly, "I don't like to gossip, Polly, as you know, but I do believe that Frank DiCaccio has moved in with her, now that Jackson has disappeared."

"What about Frank's wife? He's married to that thin good-looking younger woman, isn't he?"

"I believe she's still in the villa they bought last year, over on Osprey Street."

They had completed their walk around the lake and come back to Fran's place, so Polly turned in there, leaving the story of Ginger and Frank DiCaccio in the realm of mystery.

"I won't bother Fran with that gossip," Polly thought. "She's so committed to the idea of marriage that she won't like hearing about this kind of a mess." She remembered how, so many years ago, Fran had argued that Polly should try to save her marriage, at the time when Polly's mother and father wanted her to leave Harold. Then Harold himself had left, and Fran had appeared more devastated than Polly herself. Better leave that bit of gossip about Ginger's troubled marriage aside.

Nor could she fill Fran in on what concerned her more right now, the visit this weekend of Gerald's daughter. She had not heard from him yet, but presumably he would phone tomorrow night with some report.

He offered no details, as it turned out, just a dismissal of the visit as "pointless." "My fault," he said. "I couldn't tell her how I feel."

"About her, you mean?"

"About you." He said a hurried goodnight and hung up.

Again, nothing she could report to Fran.

Next day at Coffee-Cuppers Gerald joined Polly in the lineup, making no reference to his last call, but suggesting crisply that after visiting Fran later in the afternoon they should drive together to the beach to watch the sunset. "John says there are always cars lined up there at sundown," he had said.

"I know," Polly had answered. "People stand on the beach and clap when the last bit of the sun disappears over the water. Very dramatic!" He nodded and dropped bak to his usual table, leaving her free to join Irma, Ginger and the Vanderburgs.

Irma reported, on the way home from Coffee-Cuppers, that Saturday's church service had been quite pleasant, quite pleasant indeed. Lots of nice hymns. The flowers were beautiful.

"And no incense?" Polly laughed.

"No, no incense." Then Irma blurted out, "But it's not the incense I really object to about the Catholics. It's the Pope!"

"But he's a long way away, you know, Irma."

"Yes of course." They strolled on a little further before Irma continued, "And when the soloist sang 'I know that my Redeemer lives' I realized that basically everyone believes the same thing, whatever religion they are."

"Oh, Irma," Polly couldn't resist. "What about Buddhists and Muslims and Hindus?"

Irma had a ready answer. "Oh well, heathens, of course not. Anyway, Bill and I agree about the really important things: abortion, chastity—"

This time Polly stifled her laughter. "Those things don't seem really urgent at our stage in life," she said.

Irma was horrified. "It's the principle of the thing!"

Polly let the dangerous topic drop. She was too delighted to hear that Irma's first venture into the orbit of popery had gone off relatively calmly.

Many hours later, as she stood with Gerald facing the sunset show of clouds and water, each moment more colorful than the last, Polly told him about Irma, sitting in church with Bill on Saturday, grateful for the absence of incense, and thinking about the "really important things."

Gerald simply said "Ha!" and turned back to the darkening sky.

She saw very little of Bill in the next few days. He seemed to have given up (temporarily at least) the joy of golf for the pleasure of shuffleboard with Irma. Polly was not surprised to hear that his daughter Lorraine was going to fly down for a quick weekend visit.

On the morning after her arrival, Lorraine waved a friendly hello to Polly, and then strode away in the direction of Irma's villa. Bill, coming out to water his gardenias, explained to Polly, where she knelt, dead-heading the turbulent growth in her own garden, "Loraine thought she should explain a bit more to Irma about the church, now that she's taking an interest." He added, "Both my girls like Irma, you know."

Polly couldn't wait to tell Fran and Carl about this development; Gerald too. In fact, this was probably the time to bring her oldest friends and her newest one together. "I'll have a dinner party," she thought happily, forgetting her four-year-ago vow of abstinence from hospitality. "Maybe Friday. Lorraine will be gone, so I can ask Irma and Bill —"

When she phoned Irma with her invitation, Polly couldn't resist asking, "What does your own family think about your going around with Bill?" (She couldn't think of any more appropriate phrase than "going around with" – the language of her youth.)

Irma was unfazed. "They couldn't care less. They're so far away, you know. We rarely get together any more. I think of people in Palm Haven as my family now."

Five friends assembled on Friday – but no Irma. Polly had planned to serve a bland pasta dish, in honor of Fran's recuperating state, so she could hold back the dinner for a while. Eventually, however, Bill said, "She is sometimes forgetful," so Polly phoned to remind her.

Horrified   apologies.   "Completely   forgot   about
it...remembered this morning, and I ironed my blue blouse . . . so
sorry . . . I'll be there in ten minutes, if you will still have me!"

"Of course!"

Bill said, to no one in particular, "She's such a dear. She *is*
forgetful though, poor little thing – needs someone to look after
her."

So Irma had two strings to her bow, Polly thought: prettiness
and pathos. "Whereas," she thought, as she stirred the sauce into
the cannelloni, "Whereas I have no such strings. And no bow, for
that matter. And certainly no beau!" She laughed at herself for
letting the old term slip into her mind. Certainly Gerald Switzer
was far removed from anyone's notion of a beau. He was scowling
unaffectedly when Irma fluttered in. Polly looked at him with
amusement. With affection too. His directness was a welcome
contrast to Irma's airs and graces. Her party was going well, if you
defined "well" as consisting of a mixed group of people, all willing
to enjoy a meal together, and prepared to differ from one on other
on virtually any conceivable topic.

All in all, the party had lifted her spirits. She realized as she
finished putting the dishes into the dish washer that she had been

tired through and through from a week of trying to help Carl organize his house so as to make things as easy as possible for Frances.

She had been depressed, too, as some unfocused sadness seeped into her consciousness. Maybe it was the sight of the birds flocking together in preparation for northern flight, the annual renewal that she would never experience again. Soon the human snowbirds would be flocking toward six months of spring and summer in northern Michigan, or the Finger Lakes, or the Adirondacks. Carl was already beginning to prepare for their trip north to visit the elder son Lars. This year Fran had to leave all the preparations to him, so he was climbing the ladder into the loft to bring down the suitcases, doing extra washing and sorting, organizing food supplies so that they could "eat their way out of the place." Carl was working too hard, under a strain to do the work he had always shared with Fran.

Polly too would soon be preparing to leave Florida, but for a briefer time, and with less sense of excitement each year, as the grandchildren grew older, less interested in her presence. Tansy and Hal and herself, the old threesome that had survived so many vicissitudes together, had become less close to each other. She had the sense of something conspiratorial in the way her son and daughter eyed her life, her health and her friends. She dreaded the coming time when she would probably have to depend on Tansy and Hal more than she ever had in the past. Certainly neither of them depended on her anymore. Changes would come, and of course not for the better. She stepped outside into her darkening garden.

-13-   *SUNSHINE BRIDGE*

Gerald, as he left her house, had said, "Tomorrow I will call for you just before sunset again. If convenient."

She had said, "Quite convenient, thank you." She smiled now, remembering, and thinking, "That's the opposite of change: someone you hardly know begins to sound so familiar. 'If convenient,' indeed!"

As she turned back into her house, the Bottle-Brush tree that so recently flaunted spring chandeliers of scarlet blossoms was suddenly black with crows, crowding onto a shared perch as they prepared to swoop away north. In an instant they were up and away. Over by Bill's house, the satiny green of his buttonwood was similarly masked, and another flock, of finches this time, settled in a green-gold cloud on a low-cut laurel. As quickly as they had come together, they too were gone.

At the edge of the patio the tall gray-blue heron stood poised, the sinuous neck perfectly still. Then like lightning a sudden thrust, and a swift gecko, not swift enough, was scissored and flipped up into the heron's strong golden beak.

That very night Frances phoned in the middle of the night, her voice almost impossible to understand. "Polly. Carl —"

Polly said "I'll come right away. Hang on Fran," Fran's voice sounded dreadful. Of course she was still very weak from her operation, but there was a different kind of panic in her tone.

Carl was slumped by the bedroom door, doubled up, obviously in pain. "I'll call Gerald," Polly said, and in the next breath, "No, I'll dial 911."

Carl had suffered a massive coronary attack. By the time the ambulance came he was unconscious. By the time they reached the hospital, with incredible finality, he was dead.

At midnight Polly faced the dreadful job of phoning Lars and Norman, to tell them of their father's death. Gerald had given Fran a sedative, in spite of her objections. "You have a bad day to get through tomorrow," he said. "Much better to get some rest, even unnatural rest, tonight." Fran had seemed too stunned to resist. Polly was prepared to refuse if Gerald offered her the same panacea, but he seemed to assume that she had not the same need for momentary forgetfulness. He assumed, too, that it would be her job to phone Lars and Norman. For once, it seemed easy to accept his directions. She did the phoning, and shared the desolation.

At a sleepless daybreak Polly called Tansy, and Tansy said, "I'll come, Mother. Of course I'll come. This morning, if I can get a flight. I'll cancel appointments for a couple of days. Oh, poor, poor Aunt Fran!" Then Polly had to repeat the same sad process with Hal; he too promised to come, by evening for sure, earlier if possible.

How to pick them all up? Problem partly solved by the Andersen sons, who phoned back to say they would rent a car in Tampa, so as to have extra transportation available. That left Tansy and Hal: another problem, this time solved by Gerald. No point in staying with Fran this morning, he announced, in an early morning phone message: the sedative would keep her groggy until early afternoon. He would cope with the airport pickup, he promised. By noon, he and Polly were on their silent way to Tampa.

Tansy came out of the airport elevator, but stopped short when the doctor took the carry-on out of her hand. She firmly seized it back, and extended a very cold hand and a very stiff smile to him.

He spoke sharply in his best pediatrician's manner: "Now, Tansy, you must try to be more friendly to me. Your mother and I are working together to help Frances."

Polly gasped. No one had spoken to strong-willed Tansy in that tone since she was a very small girl. Tansy's response was instant: "Just because you boss my mother around doesn't mean you can tell me what to do!"

"Boss your mother? I certainly would not dream of doing that!" Then, "Well, perhaps in a professional situation, at the clinic."

"I'm not talking about the clinic!" Mercifully, however, along with the strong will Tansy had inherited some of her mother's sense of humor. Her smile turned suddenly warmer, and she held out her hand again. "Is this better?"

The smile disappeared as she turned to hug her mother and cry, "But Uncle Carl!"

On the way back to Palm Haven, Polly talked compulsively to Tansy. Anything to avoid another clash. She pointed out the oleanders, the Sunshine Bridge, the jacaranda, the osprey nest at the top of an tall dead pine. Finally she talked about the funeral arrangements. There would be a minimal ceremony tomorrow at the funeral parlor, no reception afterwards, just the family coming back with Fran to the house. Along with the Andersen sons and the grandchildren, Tansy and Hal constituted "family" in one sense. They had known the Andersen boys since childhood, and had come to love Fran's daughters-in-law and grandchildren. Nevertheless, it would not be appropriate to go straight to Fran's house now. Her sons needed time with her alone, and they would have arrived by this time.

A few hours remained before going back to the airport (St. Petersburg this time) to meet Hal. Gerald disappeared at this point, promising to return in lots of time for the next pick up. Tansy and Polly sat down to a cold lunch and a desultory chat. By silent agreement, they avoided discussing Polly's affairs at first, and drifted into reminiscences of long-ago times, when the two young families had spent holidays together, Carl as the father figure to the whole gang, once Harold had left. Over the years, Tansy had never found it easy to go back to those memories but now she seemed released into quiet talk even about the long-tabooed subject of her father.

She slipped back into her strong-minded norm just before it was time to go for Hal. "You really must do something about this place, Mother. I don't think you've changed a thing here since you moved in. You just dumped all your stuff in with all the furniture that came with the house."

"Yes, well, as soon as I got here, Fran had ideas for things we should do together. I just left everything as it was and started my new life here."

"Now that you're thoroughly established in your life here, surely you could organize your house a bit better?"

"I kind of like my mess," Polly said defensively, but she felt that she hadn't heard the last of this subject now that Tansy had actually seen how she lived. Incredibly, Tansy had never been here in the villa since the weekend when she helped with the moving in. Weekly chats were fine, and the annual holiday visits up north even finer, but Tansy had lost the close connection with her mother that had made the early years bearable for both of them. Polly looked at her comfortable clutter, the confusion in her house, with new eyes.

No wonder Tansy was critical. The house showed the way she had been drifting through the years here. What on earth would Tansy say if she knew about the way she was drifting now into a confused relationship with Gerald, an opening out into confidences on his part, and a flush of sympathy and – yes – affection on her own?

Tansy had not finished giving directions. "You simply must buy a proper dress for tomorrow. You can't go to a funeral in one of those washed-out T-shirts and baggy jeans, and it's much too hot for your black pant-suit." Yes, in the evening they would go to De Soto Mall and find something. Would Hal come with them? Probably not; but Hal had always been able to make himself comfortable wherever he was. Regardless, before thinking about shopping she would go sit with Fran this afternoon, dressed as her ordinary self, to be with Fran in her extraordinary sorrow.

The morning of the funeral was beautiful and sunny. "It really is glorious weather, isn't it?" Tansy mused, as if she had never quite believed her mother's reports on the wonders of a Florida spring.

Amy Malone phoned. "John and I won't be there, but you know we will be thinking of you. And I would so much like to meet your son and daughter. Could I drop in for a brief visit when the funeral is over? Or would you all come by here?"

Polly thought that was the better alternative. The prospect of anyone dropping into her house in its present chaotic state would probably send Tansy into a tizzy. "We'll drop in."

So now it was time to don the new dress and get over to the funeral home.

Fran and Carl's grandchildren, awed as they were, and touched by sorrow, still humanized the funeral ceremony and the little get-together afterwards. They swarmed around "Aunt Tansy" and "Uncle Hal" demanding news of their young people, and they made polite overtures to Gerald Switzer, the only stranger in the midst of the family. At the edge of the increasingly lively chatter, Fran sat silent and miserable, eating what they gave her, accepting a drink. "Scotch, Mom. Good for you."

Lars said quietly to Polly, "Of course it's dreadful for Mom. But think of Dad – no long illness, no having to depend on anyone to look after him. We should be grateful. He knew, I think. His father went the same way, and his grandfather too, and at about the same age."

It should have been a consolation. To Fran, sitting in the lanai, looking at the lake and the wheeling gulls as the sun went down, there was clearly no comfort.

A subdued foursome walked up the path to the Malones' house. Gerald opened the door and stiffly gestured to Polly to lead the way in. Stiffness disappeared in the warm welcome proffered by Amy and John: they seemed to assume that Tansy and Hal were their friends, in need of extra comfort today. By the end of a quiet hour in the lanai, the tensions of the day relaxed. Gerald, as always when Amy was around, seemed gentle and at ease. Polly surprised herself by the little surge of pleasure that came from listening to him and Hal renewing their friendly exchange of linguistic ideas, and drawing John into their discussion. Even Tansy softened a bit in talking to Amy, though she clearly was keeping a professional eye on the way her mother warmed to Gerald's friends.

As they were leaving, Amy drew Polly aside and said quietly, "John and I haven't wanted to talk about it when we were all together but we are so very sorry about Carl. It's so hard to believe anything so drastic could happen so suddenly, without any warning." Her voice darkened. "We are truly concerned about Fran. I didn't know her well, of course, but Rusty has talked to me about her a lot these last few weeks and I have looking forward to knowing her better. Now, I wonder what she plans to do. Will she stay on in Palm Haven alone?"

An astonishing question, one that had never crossed Polly's mind. Her amazement must have shown in her face, because Amy quickly caught herself up and explained. "That's a silly question, I guess, for someone as strong as Fran. In spite of her recent bout she is obviously an undaunted person. But I suppose I asked, because I know I couldn't live here without John. We barely make it as it is." She was doing her best to smile, and that made it easy for Polly to pick up a social tone and say a sincere thank you for a nice time. "A healing time for all of us," she said. In truth, she could see how some of their grief seemed to have lifted from Hal and Tansy in the process of the quiet friendly visit.

Tansy and Hal left that same night, taken in a single trip to their respective airports. Gerald pulled up first at the Departure entrance in Tampa, leaving Polly and her son and daughter alone while he went to park the car. Tansy, her briskness restored, seized the opportunity to speak swiftly: "Now, Mother, don't let that man dominate you. I can see he is really becoming part of your everyday life. If you go on seeing him he may even try to bulldoze you into marrying him. If you were my client I would tell you to consider very carefully, your goals, your values."

Polly said slowly, "I can do with some advice, Tansy, so I do thank you. Gerald hasn't the slightest notion of marrying me. But I do enjoy his company."

Tansy responded. "I can see that. My best advice would be that you should try living together for a while."

In Polly's mind a giggly voice said, "What would poor Gerald think of *that* suggestion?"

Tansy was sailing on, "A better option in my opinion. That way you could back out without consequences."

"Consequences?"

"Financial. Legal."

"Is that the modern version of marriage counseling? Good heavens!" Old memories surfaced. "When I think how upset I was when you moved in with James, before you were married – " (Upset? No; devastated, embarrassed . . .)

Tansy answered with a superior smile, "Attitudes change. Anyway, you weren't nearly as concerned a few years later when Hal and Mona began living together. My advice is –"

No time for more advice, acceptable or otherwise; Gerald rejoined them, smiling amiably, presumably believing he had mollified Tansy by carefully refraining from directing any further orders at her. After she went to the departure line, it was time to go to the other airport with Hal, who had stood aside while Tansy delivered her advice, as he so often had in the past. He kissed his mother, gave her an extra hug and said, "It's so lucky for Aunt Fran that you're right here. But I do know how you'll miss Uncle Carl. 'My Consultant,' you used to call him." He couldn't quite manage a laugh at the old joke.

"But I've still got 'My Rock'," Polly said, and hugged him back.

Gerald drove in silence most of the way home. Polly saw no need for chatter about oleanders, jacarandas, osprey nest or anything else.

Silence was the norm for the next few days. Fran, dry-eyed, had retreated completely into herself. Polly tried to get her out and about, dropped in on the way to Coffee-Cuppers, tried to get her to come to the chorale concert, or to turn out for bridge. Giving up on these organized affairs, she tried just to get Fran to come over for tea, for a light lunch, for a drink. Nothing. Fran was sitting in the dark most of the time, with the drapes pulled across the beautiful view of the lake.

"Can't I help you any way?" Polly asked in despair, in the second week after Carl's death. Now that Lars and Norman had returned to Indiana, Fran seemed more lost than ever.

Fran broke her silence. "I don't think so, Polly. Thank you. I don't sleep. I've slept beside that nice warm body for forty-five years, and I just can't seem to get sleepy on my own."   Wonder of wonders, the old laughing Fran seemed to be breaking through for a moment or so. Polly seized the opening and asked about sleeping pills.

"No, they just seem to make me fuzzy for about fifteen minutes, and then I'm wide awake, with a headache on top of –"

"On top of heart-ache. Of course. Hot drinks? A little scotch and hot water?"

"Maybe." Dreamily Fran went on. "Scotch. You know my family was Scottish. Carl's family came originally from Sweden of course, but mine came from Aberdeen. Nowadays I hear in my head all the old Scotch love songs that my grandmother used to sing." Fran's soft voice lifted into a little whisper of song: "*How can ye chaunt, ye warbling birds, When I'm so weary, full of care?*"

Polly sat, silenced. Fran went on: "Another one I can't stop running through my mind is 'John Anderson, my jo, John.' In my mind I change it to `Carl Anderson, my jo, Carl.' I sing it inside my head all the time. Silly!" For the first time, Fran was crying.

"Not silly!" Polly protested. "Dear Fran, I guess all this is the price you pay for having had such a good marriage."

Fran was dabbing at her tears with shaky finger-tips. "Sorry, Polly, I've tried everything, and nothing works."

Indeed nothing did work, except the canker of loneliness, that ate into Fran's life.

Her son Lars came back to Florida, to try to comfort her. In desperation, Lars said to Polly, "We think we will try to get Mom to move back to Indiana, to be near one or other of us. There are nice retirement places, if she doesn't want to actually live with us. I'm sure she would find it easier to accept Dad's death if she were near us, especially the grandchildren. I believe she's thinking about selling and coming home."

Of course the possibility had crossed Polly's mind since Amy mentioned it, but it was a shock to hear it put into words as a real potential decision.

Fran, however, wouldn't hear of such a scheme, for the present at least. "This is where Carl and I planned to stay forever. This has been the happy place. You know that, Polly. Here at Palm Haven I have you. I couldn't bear to be separated from you, too."

Walking home, Polly thought of all the times she and Fran had strolled this path, in twilight, watching reflections glow on the silver lamé surface. "The long light shakes across the lake," Fran had quoted, from the poetry they had memorized together in school. Now dark fingers stretched to the east horizon, pulling down the dark blind of night. In the west the last shafts of sunlight turned the silver lake, briefly, to gold.

Two days later, Fran's second son, Norman, returned to Florida to take his turn at persuading his mother to give up her Florida home. This time Fran produced a new twist to the idea of selling the villa and moving back up north. "Polly, what would you think if we both sold and went back home together?"

Polly was taken aback. "Indiana's not home to me any more, Fran," she protested. "Neither Tansy or Hal is there. It's different for you. You'd have your sons and grandchildren."

"Having you seems to matter more right now. I couldn't talk to the young people. Couldn't gossip with them. They don't remember the right things!" Obviously Fran was sufficiently perked up by her idea to tease her son a little. "We could have fun together, Poll. For a few years at least."

Norman intervened. "Polly needs time to think about your idea, Mom."

Indeed she did. She was restless and unsettled. But the thought of Indiana, even with Fran, brought no peace.

-14-   *ANHINGA*

Next morning, Polly was sitting on her patio sadly nursing a cup of coffee when a cheerful "Hi, there!" announced Ginger Elrick. This time, Polly invited her into the house. All the old defenses of her privacy seemed to be dissolving.

Ginger dropped into one of Polly's lanai chairs, asking for news of Fran, of course, but also announcing her own news. "You know about Jackson pulling out, Polly?"

Polly nodded. Everyone knew that Ginger was alone in the villa at the head of the lake. Well, nearly alone. Everyone also seemed to know that Frank DiCaccio had become a constant visitor there, doing who knew what. Everyone was sorry for his wife, alone in her villa at the other end.

In fact, as so often at Palm Haven, what everyone knew was not in fact the case. Ginger explained, "Frank and I have had to spend a lot of time together. We had blocked out the basic changes in our decorating scheme, but it has taken ages to get the details fleshed out. Thank goodness it's almost over!"

"I suppose it's been fun in a way?"

"Far from it! Frank is the most opinionated man I have ever known. And I have known a lot of opinionated men, believe me! When this job is over I hope never to see him again in my life!"

Polly rallied from this shock and asked, "You will stay on here, though, won't you?"

"Probably." It turned out that Ginger was thinking of starting her own business but not sure whether she could run it effectively from Palm Haven.

"What business?"

"Decorating. I picked up a lot of good ideas off of Frank, even if I found him unbearable to work with. He's convinced me that within a very little while all sorts of people who retired to Florida and slotted into the pale so-called 'Florida style' will want to change. Especially the younger ones. They'll be ready to go with the darker earth colors, Italian colors: umber, sienna, olive, Pompeii red. You know."

Polly didn't know, but Ginger sailed on. "For instance, I could give you some great ideas for changing your place here, Polly. To start with, if you don't mind my saying so, those faded chintz drapes should go, and some of these chairs."

"Tansy said the same thing."

"Let's do it!" Before Polly had really decided, the drapes were down, shaken, folded, and destined for Goodwill. "And the chairs – that whole extra patio set could go to the Salvation Army. They're collecting for the Mexican migrant workers. And that extra little cupboard."

Polly's first panicky thought was "If only Fran were herself, she would tell me if this is a good idea." Fran or no Fran, it was clearly an improvement to have the drapes down. The living room seemed full of light.

The walls now looked strangely drab, though, without the chintz. "Maybe I should get some paint."

"Indeed!" Ginger was in full spate. "I know just the right thing to do with the walls. And the floor, You really need to replace that rug with tiles, Italian ones."

This was going too far. "I really can't afford such changes, Ginger."

Ginger replied with a proposal. "Let me decorate for you, and then use your place as a sort of show-piece, to get other clients."

That was not an idea compatible with Polly's pride.

Ginger's visit ended with a stalemate. Polly's house stood minus drapes, exposed to the need for further change.

Visiting Fran late in the afternoon, Polly recounted the conversation. Fran showed very little interest.

Gerald, dropping in to join her and Fran at the end of his day at the clinic, was similarly unimpressed. A decorator's skill, obviously, was no more exciting to him when it was directed at Polly's place than it had been when it involved his own villa. He was only mildly interested in the other part of Polly's news about Ginger. "It seems that the house here is her own. She bought it, not Jackson. She can stay on and work from home, when she starts her business. She's only sixty-three, and so full of energy. I don't see why she shouldn't go into this enterprise and make a go of it."

"Possibly so," was as far as Gerald would go on that topic.

Fran contributed nothing. Even the breakdown of Ginger's marriage hardly caught her attention. Polly thought it would be wise not to mention her own suspicion that the "marriage" had perhaps never actually existed. No one would have asked Ginger and Jackson to prove they were married when they bought property here (although the condominium constitution was specific on that topic: married couples only, no children, no pets). Certainly Ginger was very breezy about Jackson's departure.

At Coffee-Cuppers Irma announced, "Ginger says I should see her plans for your house, Polly. She is going to do my place too. This way, if Bill and I ever decide to marry we would have a home that is new for both of us."

Bill, who had temporarily at least renounced his Monday morning golf date in favor of Coffee-Cuppers with Irma and her friends, nodded fondly. (Polly thought a little sadly that Gerald had not joined the group and probably never would join it.)

"You girls are just reacting to the nesting instinct," was the laughing comment of Theo Vanderburg. "Just like the birds, picking up a choice bit of grass or a twig."

Polly laughed. "For me, it seems to be an *un*-nesting instinct. I'm taking apart the nest I organized when I first came here to Florida."

Ginger reacted more vigorously. "Not a nesting instinct at all! It's a question of rational choice. Birds fly south by instinct and build their nests by instinct. We *choose* to come south, for logical reasons, no ice, no winter clothes."

"Golf all year round, almost," Bill chimed in.

Ginger swept on. "This is our chosen habitat. We settle here and choose how to enrich it, make it more comfortable and more stylish. Not like the birds at all." She concluded, "I'm a great believer in choice!" She seemed to be indirectly defending her own new choice of a solitary life – after two (or maybe three?) experiences with the mating instinct.

Theo Vanderburg argued, "Life is not directed by choice, but by luck. We were lucky enough to afford the choice of Florida retirement. Chance can sweep it all away. Look at the hurricane last fall, suddenly destroying the habitat of all the folks at Pelican Key!"

Polly added silently, "And the hurricane of death that swept away Fran's happiness."

Chance; choice; instinct; luck: topics too big for a quiet Monday morning. She had better get back to her own little habitat and think about her own imminent choice, about reorganizing her house.

As she left the clubhouse, John Malone loped over to speak to her. "Amy is afraid she spoke out of turn when you were at our place," he said. "She feels she shouldn't have mentioned the possibility of Fran leaving Palm Haven. None of her business, she says, and foolishly upsetting for you to have to think of any such remote possibility."

"Not remote," Polly answered sadly. "Fran is indeed turning it over in her mind. Her sons want her to go back to Indiana. In fact –" she tried for a lighter tone, "They want to pack me up and move me there with her. And just when I'm considering redecorating my own messy house here! I'd have trouble selling it as is, that's for sure."

John's laugh was a little forced. "I hope never to hear about decorating or redecorating again, myself," he said. "But seriously, would you find time to drop in and see Amy some time soon? She's feeling remorseful about troubling you." He added a cheerful goodbye.

An anhinga, the torpedo bird, seemed to be swimming on the surface of the lake, in concert with Polly as she continued on her way from the clubhouse. Then suddenly it was gone, submerged without trace. How long could it stay beneath the water? Polly counted to twenty, with still no sign of the sleek black head. Suddenly her eye was caught by a flick of movement way out on the lake, in the opposite direction from where she had been looking. There it was. What had it been doing beneath the water? What path of current had turned it in a new direction? Had it chosen to switch directions? How little we know about the birds, even though we watch them daily, Polly thought; watch them, but never understand them.

She went indoors briefly. When she came out again, intent on going first to Fran's and then to Amy's, the anhinga was in sight again. Now it was perched high up in the Tree of Gold right in front of her house, spreading its angular wings to catch the wind and the sun.

The visit to Fran followed a pattern: Polly chatting away about Irma and Bill, Ginger and

Jackson, and about Theo Vanderburg holding forth on the topic of chance. All without rousing Fran, who sat today at her dining-room table, hands clasped in front of her. A brief visit, and then on the Malones, to see Amy.

The front door was ajar. Amy called from her corner of the sofa to come in, and launched at once into the apology for tactlessness on the day of the funeral. Brushing that aside, Polly said, "It was good you forewarned me. Fran really is talking about moving to Indiana. But I'm really here to pick up your library books. They're due, and so are mine. I'll take them in. But I wondered if you would like me to charge out the ones I've been reading, so you could see if you enjoy them as much as I have. Rose Tremaine, Penelope Fitzgerald – I thought of you when I was reading them and I bet you'd enjoy them."

"And that would save me from making the trip to the library. Very thoughtful!" Amy gestured to the pile of library books on her coffee table. "You might want to do the same thing: get them to charge mine out to you. They were all fine, except for *Amsterdam* – too tough for me. You might like it though." They settled quickly into a book-talk, with mutual pleasure.

As she finally walked toward her house, Polly saw Millicent Morgan, across the road, standing at her mailbox. "Come over for a moment," she called.

Before Polly was half way across the road, Millie was launched. "I hear your friend Ginger has thrown over both her husband and her boyfriend! And Irma Beaton has snaffled Bill Magee. Too bad! He would have been a good friend for Fran Andersen, now that she is alone."

Polly gasped. Sweet, silly Bill, and wise, witty Fran – not even the keenest gossip-knitters of Palm Haven could hook that pair into a romantic item! "I must pick up my own mail and get a little lunch," she announced, and snaked off across the road.

Later that afternoon, Gerald pulled into the drive. It was time for sunset and the little ritual that had established itself. As they drove again toward Coquina Beach, Polly recounted the latest news, as distorted by Millie. No comment. She went on to a softer report on Amy, and on their happy switch of books. "And I must get to the library myself tomorrow at the latest." Still no comment.

Gerald silently pulled into the Coquina parking lot. Maneuvered his car into the exact same spot facing the beach as on the previous time. Another bit of instant tradition, she thought.

But something new, very new, was to be added today.

Even after he had parked, Gerald's fists were clenched on the steering wheel. Instead of getting out of the car he sat on, rigid and silent.

Then, suddenly, explosively, he half turned toward her and blurted out. "Why – *why* did you make me love you so much?"

Polly sat perfectly still. Then she felt something burst within her. "So *that's* what has been wrong with me all this time!" she cried.

He sat up very straight. "What do you mean, wrong with you? And `all this time', what does that mean? Do you mean all the time since we first worked together at the clinic? What was wrong with that?"

"Nothing! It was right! Everything is perfectly right!" She felt a blissful warmth rising. Goodness, it was love! She was flooded with the realization that her solitude had been finally breached. She had built a wall of self-mockery and self-sufficiency around herself after Harold left her, yet all that time she must have been needing love, needing to be in love. All she could say now was, "Nothing's wrong! Oh, nothing's wrong! I do love you!" and she turned toward Gerald expecting to be kissed.

His sat stiffly and his voice was stern. "I assume you will want me to marry you."

A gasp or a giggle: what was the right response to that? "Is that a proposal?" she cried. Then she answered, "No, I don't expect you to marry me. What an awful thought! I just want for now to be in love with you. If you don't mind."

Abruptly he tugged open the car door, jumped out, strode around to her side of the car and pulled her out and down the beach to the shoreline. His feet crunched on tiny shells. "We mustn't miss the sunset. As planned."

She struggled not to laugh. As he moved to the shoreline he dropped her hand and said, more calmly, "I guess I do want to ask you to marry me. That is a proposal, all right."

"Thank you, but not a good idea." She was grateful for having had time to think. Now she could say slowly but decisively, though with a laugh in her voice, "You couldn't stand to live in my clutter, and I certainly don't see the two of us trying to live in your one black chair. And I couldn't cook dinner in the heart of your kitchen forest."

He was silent, obviously miffed at her mockery of his living quarters and, presumably, of his proposal. Then he said, "Please stop laughing at me. I didn't mean to blurt out my question –my proposal – "

She reached for his hand again. It was not a funny situation after all. A potentially hurtful one, indeed, potentially a moment when the good early stages of a real friendship might be in jeopardy. "Yes, we'll talk. We mustn't stop talking. You mustn't go into one of your silences."

That made him even huffier. "I do not consider myself a particularly silent person. I do not mean to talk about – about all this – until you raise the question again yourself." He moved away from her, striding back toward the car.

In a silence such as he had just denied, he drove her back to her house and said a stiff "Goodnight". He added, "I will go with you tomorrow morning to visit Frances, of course. As planned."

Polly had indeed been thinking about Fran as they drove home. Her thought had been, "I must tell Fran about this." She had told everything to Fran for so many long years, all the way back to high school days in Indiana. Could she tell her about the "proposal" without giving way to the desire to laugh about it? Because it was not funny, not funny at all, when someone as inhibited as Gerald had burst through to a declaration of feeling, real feeling. And what could she tell Fran about her own feelings, her sense of something opening up within her? She knew what Fran's response would have been just a few weeks ago: delight. Such a romantic, Fran; so tied to a dream of everyone finding a marriage as happy as her own had been. But the new Fran – her response was unpredictable: maybe it would be indifference, maybe a little resentment of a possible happiness in a world that for her was so bleak.

All she said now as she left the car was, "About eleven o'clock then? I'll meet you there."

Next morning, at Fran's house, Gerald seemed surprisingly able to set aside the strange conversation they had had yesterday. Certainly he did a good job of chatting with Fran, as if to disprove what Polly had said yesterday about his silences. Taking her cue from him, Polly also worked hard at making conversation, trying to cheer Fran up. It seemed probable that he would simply not refer again to his strange proposal, once they were alone together.

As they walked together back toward Polly's house just before noon, he surprised her again. "I am wanting to be with you more and more," he burst out. "I keep thinking about what you said about the two of us living together in my big chair, and I have this silly great urge to be there with you. I know it's ridiculous."

"Let's go!" Polly cried. "Why should we walk along talking, here on the public road, when we could be comfortable and private and together at your place?"

He looked startled, but he turned on his heel and began to march, assuming she would fall into step with him, back along the lakeshore path toward his own house. "I've had a hard time keeping my urge to be near you under control while you've been so absorbed with Frances."

She was still laughing when he opened his lanai door and gestured her in. They passed the pile-up of rattan chairs (stacked more neatly this time by the professional movers), passed the kitchen door, spilling over with greenery. He pulled her at last into the big black leathery comfort of his solo chair. You couldn't call it snuggling, she thought: he was too bony and angular for that; but it was infinitely comfortable to feel his arms around her, his long fingers gently running through her tousle of gray curls, and to be turned around so that her head was tucked under his chin. "I do love you," she said. "Though I don't know why."

"I don't know why either. So we're a good pair, in that if in nothing else."

But in a few minutes, he said, with regret, "I'm afraid I'm hungry. We should eat, and I haven't anything in the house."

"We'll go to my place and I'll fix something," Polly answered. "You can see how you tolerate my clutter. Then we can figure out what next."

-15-   MOONLIGHT

When they turned into her drive, Bill was in his car-port, beaming at them and coming over to join them. "I hoped you'd be here in time, Polly. Irma is over at Millie Morgan's for lunch, just a girl thing. Before she went she fixed up lunch for me." His laugh rolled out, jolly and confident, "She made twice too much! She always does, bless her heart! I thought I would bring it over to your place, Polly. There's plenty for Doctor Switzer too."

"Gerald, please."

Bill looked a bit abashed, but his smile was close to the surface. "Yes. Gerald. Will you wait a minute while I collect the good things?"

"No choice!" Polly smiled, and led Gerald into her house. Her shabby belongings huddled in a crowded haphazard way in the new revealing uncurtained light. Before Gerald could comment, Bill returned, dropped the food in the kitchen, and the two men moved out to her lanai, drinks in hand. It was hard for two big men to fit in among the jumble of chairs, pulled this way and that by Ginger and left untouched since by Polly.

"Gosh, Polly," Bill exclaimed, "something has been upsetting your house! My mother would say it looks like the Wreck of the Hesperus – if you don't mind my saying so." Gerald looked as though he wouldn't mind saying a few things himself. Before he could speak, however, Bill firmly changed the subject. "Irma has gone over to tell Millie our news," he said, beaming, "so I think I have a right to tell you folks too! We are going to be married."

Gerald merely said, "Well!" but Polly cried, "Wonderful! Marvelous! When, Bill?"

His smile dimmed a bit. "Irma is taking instruction now. As soon as she is received we will set a date."

Gerald looked a bit bemused. "Received?"

Polly explained. "Into the Catholic church, Gerald. Irma is converting to Catholicism."

"Ha!" said Gerald. Religious experience obviously didn't seem a very big deal to him. "Anyway, congratulations are in order, I suppose."

Polly could see he was faintly considering telling Bill that he wasn't the only one entering into a new relationship, but he shut his mouth firmly and kept quiet.

They finished an amiable meal together, then Bill left, going across the road to pick up Irma and tell her that the lunch she prepared had been put to multiple use. (I'm not sure Irma will think that was such a great idea, Polly said to herself.) Steering around non-helpful Gerald with some difficulty, she cleared the table and set up the dish-washer.

"I don't know what to do about my house," she confessed as it started to chug. "Ginger caused all this chaos in about half an hour. What will happen when she starts in full time? I'm afraid she's going to want to get rid of the few things I really care about." She gestured toward her grandmother's love seat and the nest of little tables. "Those, for instance."

Gerald, still obviously bemused by the mess, said, tentatively, "You could store what you really like at my place, Polly. " Then he warmed to his own idea. "We could move your bits and pieces and leave the rest for Ginger to cope with. If she did a good job of redecorating you could sell this place for a good profit."

Polly, in spite of having listened to the wisdom of the investment expert, had no special interest in the good profit. "I don't want to sell."

He wasn't listening. "I'll clear out all my furniture," he offered. "That will make room for your things."

"But what about your sons? They went to the trouble of arranging for your decorator. What would they say?"

"If I can find the courage to tell them I love you, I should surely be able to tell them that I don't want to live with the decorator's ideas any longer."

That raised a new question. "When will you tell them? About us, I mean?"

A slow blush began to rise. "Actually, I phoned them both last night. They both gave me advice. Graham – he's the accountant, you know –" (Polly nodded) " Graham says that marriage is not a good option, tax-wise. And David – the lawyer, you know," (another nod from Polly) "David has a lot to say about the trust and the will and all that. He also advises against marriage, from a legal point of view."

A little silence. Finally Polly swallowed and said, "So?"

"So I decided I want to marry you, Polly. They helped me make up my mind. I would like to marry you as soon as possible."

She couldn't resist a little joke. "Even if not convenient, from your children's point of view?"

It was not a joking matter to him.

She tried to distract him. "Maybe it would be easier all round if we just go on as we are. You in your small corner, and I – in my god-awful mess."

"Don't laugh, Polly," he said. "I really want a clean sweep. I see clearly how to arrange my place. We'll have to keep my big black chair – "

Better go along with him, she thought, and added an obvious suggestion: "And your sound system."

He smiled and chimed in, "We'll move the big chair and a couple of speakers out into the lanai, so that we can look at the lake and listen to music at the same time."

How could he possibly expect to accomplish such changes? She decided, a little sourly, that being wealthy was a very big help. Then, returning to a more charitable mood, she said, "You would keep the painting of you and your children."

"And I'll need a desk for you to work at, on the whooping-cough project."

She had forgotten the whooping-cough project. But he had been recalled to business by his own words. "Good heavens! I must go. It's my afternoon at the clinic. I don't suppose –?"

"No," she said firmly.

He left it at that, told her he'd be back at supper time, and prepared to leave. But her mind had started on a different tack. He might muster courage to announce their plans to his sons, but how would she tell Tansy? Hal would not be a problem, she assumed, but Tansy –   "When Tansy was here she suggested we should just live together. That was before I was even thinking about you in this way."

Gerald's face showed as much horror at that suggestion as she had expected. "I want to marry you, Polly," he announced. "But now I must leave." And he left.

She had forgotten to ask him whether he had also phoned his daughter last night. "I'll ask first thing this evening," she thought. Amazing to realize he had already phoned his sons. But she herself felt that if there was any announcing to be done, it was Fran who should have been first to   hear about these emotional developments. "We'll go see her this evening anyway," she decided.

When Gerald came back, hot and tired from his time at the clinic, she handed him a drink and told him her feeling about Fran. "She doesn't know at all how I have come to feel about you. This is such a gossipy place, someone will be seeing us together, at the beach, maybe, and jumping to conclusions. If it's all right with you, I would like to tell Fran."

"I'm not sure exactly what we can tell her. You haven't really answered my proposal of marriage, you know." Before she could parry that, he went on, "However I think something to distract Frances would be a good idea, possibly very beneficial to her emotional state."

"Well, for goodness sakes!" Polly hadn't thought that the news about their sudden plunge into elderly romance could be regarded as a possible help for Fran.

She had one more thing to say before they set out to Fran's house. "I think you should phone your daughter. You should invite her to come back and meet me this time. Maybe we could find a way to patch up a bad relationship."

"Well, actually," he looked away, over her head, "actually I did phone her, after I talked to the boys. Her reaction was to remind me that my estate is tied up in a trust. She says she'll sue, if I change my will. Not that she needs to worry, and not that she needs whatever comes to her on my death, or would miss anything I might spend elsewhere."

"On me, you mean."

"Yes. That's what she means at least." He stood up. "I didn't do a good job of explaining to her, how I feel about her, or about you." He took a deep breath. "It is not easy for me to show my feelings. I promise to try harder with you. I can't fail again."

"You won't," she said.

They walked toward Fran's darkened house. The weather was getting very hot now, edging toward a Florida summer, somewhere in the high 80s, even well after sunset. Far away to the north an airplane rose, taking its departure from Tampa, a huge mechanical snowbird, taking people to the cooler north. "Soon I'll be on my way up north too," said Polly, thinking of the freshness of the Finger Lakes in up-state New York with Tansy's family, and the wild beauty of Hal's cottage in Maine.

Gerald replied, "I would rather take you somewhere else later in the summer. Portugal, maybe?"

Something to be worked out. . . . But the immediate job was telling Fran.

Polly felt shy as they rang the bell and stood at the front door. She had never come in except by the lanai, and had never, never, rung the door-bell when she was going to see Fran and Carl. Not Carl of course, this time; Fran only, now. She came from the lanai to let them in, and led them back to the lanai where they all sat in semi-darkness, looking out at the shiver of early moonlight on the lake.

But how to talk to Fran? This strange, slow-speaking Fran, this wordless straight-backed Fran, sitting motionless? Polly stumbled through a jumble of explanations and information, with footnotes from Gerald: all that had been happening, all that had been said, how Tansy and Hal felt, how Gerald's daughter had reacted, how John and Amy would be amazed.

Silence.

Then, in the dark lanai, a blessed peal of laughter from Fran, the old Fran, dissolved in giggles as she always had been when

Polly brought problems and puzzles to her. That laughter had always masked real love and a good deal of common sense.

What she said now was, "Perfect! You will drive each other crazy and enjoy each other forever!" Her voice dropped. "Almost forever." Then she started on a totally new, totally unexpected tack: "You two will solve my problems too. Of course I will have to stay here in my own house if you two are going to wrap yourselves around a love affair."

"What?" A simultaneous cry from both of them.

Fran giggled again, a feeble giggle, almost as though she had forgotten how to produce her old real laughter. "I will have to stay and help you, Polly! You will need practical advice about how to make a marriage work."

"Maybe not a marriage," Gerald interjected, always literal. "Polly says Tansy thinks we should just live together for a while."

"Whatever! I'll help you cope with each other! You will be my mission, helping you talk to each other, talk through your differences and problems. Neither of you is very good at talking."

Polly was indignant: "I am so, I'm good at talking! I talk all the time!"

"No, you chatter all the time, Polly darling. But you don't say what you think. You just babble on, you know you do! And behind the chatter you're just as private as Gerald is. You say something funny to hide what you really feel." It was said with such affection that no offense could be taken.

Nor could they object when Fran suddenly cried, "What we need, now, is a little libation, as darling Carl would have said! Gerald, the scotch is in that decanter on the buffet. While you're getting it, you'll find the glasses in the kitchen cupboard, right above the sink."

Gerald looked a bit bemused by this enforced enlistment in the legion of men-who-help–around-the-house, but he wandered off, obviously well-intentioned. "I'm not sure which cupboard you meant," his voice trailed back after him, causing Fran to say to Polly, "You'll need lots of help domesticating him!"

Then she called out, "Over the sink, silly! Lift up your hand and turn the knob!"

Soon, drink in hand, Fran was bubbling with ideas. "I can help you cope with your young folks. You know I could always bring Tansy and Hal into line, Polly. Especially Tansy, even when you and she were at loggerheads."

Polly hated to dampen her spirits, but, "Gerald's daughter is something else, though, Fran," she said. "She sounds daunting!"

"I'll daunt *her*!" Fran said firmly; and Polly believed her. "What about your sons, Gerald? Don't you think I can bring them round?"

Gerald, looking overwhelmed by the direction of the talk, could only say, "My sons?" and then break off, unable to guess how those dignified young men would respond to Fran's fire.

"I think they'll come round," Polly said. "They seem genuinely anxious to make their father happy, even if they take inappropriate steps."

Gerald looked as though he would defend his sons, but then he remembered the way they had arranged the decoration of his house, and desisted.

"As for the Malones, of course they will be amazed. But they'll be totally delighted, as I am, I really am!"

That was the end of Fran's spurt of gaiety. The thought of delight deflated her. She relapsed over her scotch and water into silence; but it was no longer a desolate silence.

Gerald hardly noticed her lapse. He whispered to Polly, "You see? This was the right prescription. I was correct in thinking she should hear our news. She was just joking when she talked about helping us, but jokes are always significant indicators of mental status."

Polly's laughing glance answered, "Come on, my dear, forget about your professional capacity – and just rejoice!" Then she told Fran, "We haven't had anything to eat. Could you and I rustle up some spaghetti?"

Fran, roused from her reverie, slipped out to the kitchen and Polly joined her, clattering together the familiar pots and pans.

The doctor stood in the kitchen doorway watching the two of them. He began to talk about the plans he and John Malone had made for their research, and the way Polly was expected to fit in. "After you sort our data, you will make notes on anomalies, for John and me to consider." The clatter of pans stopped. He paused and seemed to hear the echo of his own words. So he added, with an astonishing big smile, "If convenient."